THE SANTA LIST

Scholastic Children's Books
An imprint of Scholastic Ltd
Euston House, 24 Eversholt Street, London, NW1 1DB, UK
Registered office: Westfield Road, Southam, Warwickshire, CV47 0RA
SCHOLASTIC and associated logos are trademarks and/or
registered trademarks of Scholastic Inc.

First published in the UK by Scholastic Ltd, 2021

Text copyright © Kieran Crowley, 2021
Cover characters and inside illustrations by James Lancett
represented by the Bright Agency © Scholastic, 2021
The right of Kieran Crowley to be identified as the author
of this work has been asserted by him.

ISBN 978 0702 30977 9

A CIP catalogue record for this book
is available from the British Library.

Printed by CPI Group (UK) Ltd, Croydon, CR0 4YY

Papers used by Scholastic Children's Books are made
from wood grown in sustainable forests.

1 3 5 7 9 10 8 6 4 2

This is a work of fiction. Names, characters, places, incidents
and dialogues are products of the author's imagination or are used
fictitiously. Any resemblance to actual people, living or dead,
events or locales is entirely coincidental.

www.scholastic.co.uk

THE SANTA LIST

KIERAN CROWLEY

ILLUSTRATED BY JAMES LANCETT

SCHOLASTIC

'Everyone loves apple tart
and new potatoes.'

In memory of Mary Leahy
Thanks for all the Sunday
dinners, for your support and
encouragement over the years,
but mostly, thanks for showing
me the importance of never
giving up.

Chapter One

It was 5.53 p.m. on a snowy Saturday before Christmas when Mrs Grough came to stay. The tree was up, the house cheerfully decorated, and the cupboards were full of treats. And Aisling had no idea that within a few days everything would go horribly wrong.

Aisling and her younger brother Joe lived in a nice house in a nice part of town and were always, always, always in trouble. So much so that since the twenty-third of October all the babysitters in town had refused to set foot in their home. Every single one of them.

1

"I have worked as a childminder for over thirty years and they are the most terrible children I have ever had the misfortune to meet," said Billy Hegarty. His hair had turned from a beautiful chestnut brown to a ghostly white after he'd spent a single night looking after them.

"I won't ever look after those two monsters, not even for a million euros," Margaret Doyle said after an extremely long weekend. She'd never babysit professionally again.

"I've had nightmares every night since I left that house," said Deirdre Sheehan, who was now terrified of butterflies and, to a lesser extent, daddy-long-legs. "I climbed Mount Everest in a snowstorm. I've been attacked by a lion. I once accidentally covered my head in honey and ran into a swarm of bees, but I'd rather go through all of that again than spend one more second with those children."

They weren't *that* terrible; they were usually quite pleasant (well, not usually, but often enough) and they could be polite when they needed to be. And, it has to be said, they were slightly better behaved than their long-haired terrier Hudson, who looked cute but spent a lot of his free time barking at his own reflection, destroying shoes or cushions or pretty much anything that happened to be lying around, and occasionally launching an attack on the television if he spotted a wildebeest on a nature programme. Wildebeests, for reasons that were never quite clear, always got on Hudson's nerves.

Most of the time, Mr Gilligan (Dad) and Ms Murphy (Mam) were too busy to punish Aisling and Joe when they behaved badly. In fact, their work lives were so hectic they rarely got to spend much time with their children at all. They ran their own business and they were always stuck in front of their computers with stressed looks on their faces, talking rapidly on their phones, and drinking endless cups of coffee. They often had to travel to meetings, which meant that Aisling and Joe got away with things that other children might not have.

But now their parents had a problem. They were due to go on a sudden emergency super-important business trip and couldn't find anyone to look after their children for a few days. Most of their family lived far away and since all their previous babysitters had refused to help, they didn't know what they were going to do. Until Dad spotted an advertisement on the internet:

Are your children too rambunctious for your ordinary, everyday babysitter? Then try:

THE GRANITE & STEEL BABYSITTING COMPANY

All of our babysitters have been in the army, are trained in karate, and can free-dive, rock climb, parachute, sew, hoover and cook.

✦ Chapter ✦ Two

This babysitting company was exactly what Aisling and Joe's parents were looking for. They needed someone strong enough to stand up to their children, someone who would take charge of the situation, but mainly they needed someone who wouldn't panic when they found their coat pockets had been filled with custard. While Mam and Dad were discussing their good fortune at finding the company, they failed to notice that Aisling and Joe were lurking on the other side of the door, listening in. They smelled trouble.

"I don't like the sound of this," Aisling whispered.

"Me neither," Joe replied. "I don't know why our old babysitters won't come back. We were never *that* bad. Anyway, it's December now. We're always good in December. Mam and Dad should know that."

This was true. Aisling and Joe always tried their best to be well-behaved in December. The last thing they wanted was to be put on Santa's List. If they were on the bad list, then there was a chance they wouldn't get any Christmas presents. And they wanted Christmas presents. They *needed* Christmas presents, and if being good was the terrible price they had to pay, then they were going to pay it.

As luck would have it, the Granite & Steel Babysitting Company had someone available, and the very next evening Mrs Grough, wearing a thick woollen coat and a pair of sensible shoes, walked up the short front drive to number seventeen, crunching along the gravel and snow. Aisling and Joe watched from an upstairs window.

"She's doesn't look that tough," Aisling said.

"Yeah, there's nothing for us to worry about," Joe replied.

The downstairs hallway was filled with the suitcases and briefcases and rolled-up charts their parents needed for their trip.

"I hate going away like this, just before Christmas," Dad said.

"I know. I'm really going to miss our two little angels," Mam said. Then she suddenly looked nervous. "Wait, they haven't booby-trapped any of our stuff, have they?"

Dad turned pale. "Like the time we went to Paris? That was a nightmare. We'd better check," he said, frantically rifling through their luggage.

As Aisling and Joe trooped downstairs, the doorbell chimed. Their mother plastered a fake smile on her face and opened the front door.

"Hello. Mrs Grough, I presume. Come in, come in, it's very cold out there."

"Cold? It's barely even minus five degrees," Mrs Grough replied in a clear, crisp tone. She stamped her feet on the brown brush *Welcome* mat to shake the snow from her shoes before stepping inside and placing her battered leather suitcase on the floor. Dad reached for the case to carry it up to her room.

"Do not touch that, please. The natural oils in your hands will damage the leather."

"Sorry. Family heirloom?"

Mrs Grough ignored the question, removed her coat and threw it across the hall, where it landed perfectly on the coat rack.

"So, ah, welcome," Dad said. He waved an arm in his children's direction. "This is Aisling and Joe. You're going to be good for Mrs Grough, aren't you?"

"Don't worry," Mrs Grough said, before

11

they had time to answer. "There's never been a child I couldn't tame."

Hudson emerged from the kitchen, tail a-wagging, and click-clacked his way across the wooden hall floor intent on greeting Mrs Grough, but her icy glare froze him halfway to his destination.

"Sit," she said. And Hudson did sit, much to Aisling and Joe's astonishment. "Why is the dog here? I told you that my babysitting company does not allow indoor pets."

"I'll take him out before we leave," Dad said, scooping the little dog up in his arms.

"What? But he prefers it in here with us. You can't put him outside, especially when it's Christmas," Aisling said.

"As far as I'm concerned, Christmas begins on Christmas Day and ends on the sixth of January. That means it will be Christmas in four days' time and not one second before then," Mrs Grough said, running a finger across the top of the hall dresser and finding far too much dust there for her liking. "Now, Ms Murphy. . ."

"You can call me Janet," Mam said.

"I can, but I won't. If you are to make your destination on time, I suggest you leave now, so I'll put the dog outside. And there's no need to worry, I will take good care of your children."

Mam and Dad managed to communicate without saying anything, which is a skill that married people who spend a lot of time together often develop.

Mam's look said: *I'm not sure I like this woman.*

Dad's look said: *She has great references and nobody's ever complained about her and let's be honest, there's absolutely no one else in the world who will willingly look after Aisling and Joe; even their own grandparents made up ridiculous excuses to avoid spending time with them. Do you really believe Grandad Gilligan can't babysit because he's snowboarding this weekend or that Granny Murphy is too busy creating her own YouTube music channel with all of her favourite heavy metal songs? And we need to go on this business trip or else our company will fail and we might have to sell everything we own.*

It was a lot to communicate with a single look, but he managed it, and less than three minutes later they bundled out the door, blowing kisses and promising their children that the next three days would whizz right by.

Then the front door clicked shut, and with it the world outside.

Mrs Grough opened her precious suitcase, took out two A4-size laminated sheets and handed one each to Aisling and Joe.

"I am aware that children these days don't

like rules, which doesn't surprise me as modern parents seem to let their offspring race around doing whatever they want like feral cats or untamed giraffes. My generation had nothing but rules and we all turned out perfectly fine. These sheets give you an idea of what I expect from you, but I shall now explain things in a lot more detail."

"It's going to be a long three days," Joe said.

Mrs Grough's Rules & Regulations for a Well-Ordered House

Wake-Up & Meals

Wake-up call: 6.30 a.m. (this is later than my usual time, as you are on school holidays)

Breakfast: 7.00 a.m. sharp – porridge made with water

Lunch: 12.15 p.m. – variety of delicious food, e.g. beetroot, cottage cheese and radish salad

Dinner: 5.30 p.m. – warm, nourishing meals, e.g. liver, onions, boiled cabbage and potatoes

Chores

Chores should be completed promptly and include but are not limited to: cleaning bathrooms, washing floors, washing dishes, laundry, taking out the rubbish.

Bedtime

7 p.m. sharp – **do not** ask to stay up later unless you want bedtime changed to 6.30 p.m.

Frequently Asked Questions

Are sweets allowed? No, sweets are bad for you. Treats include apples and oatcakes.

Can we watch television or use the internet? You will be allowed fifteen minutes of television **or** internet per day provided you have been well-behaved.

Can we use smartphones? Only adults are allowed to use phones.

What are the rules on dogs? Minimum of one hour's walk per day. Must stay outside.

No to
Loud noises, shouting, giggling foolishly, childish pranks, running indoors, playing music beyond a volume of three, chewing loudly, talking with your mouth full, belching, breaking wind, taking the stairs more than one at a time, wearing shoes indoors.

Yes to
Being respectful, playing quietly, doing extra chores without being asked.

Chapter Three

Aisling couldn't contain herself when Mrs Grough carried a slightly huffy Hudson into the back garden.

"He's an indoor dog," she cried. "You can't leave him out there. Look at his shivering little face. He'll be frozen."

"Nonsense," said Mrs Grough. "Dogs are meant to be outdoors. It'll toughen him up. I once slept on the edge of a cliff in temperatures of minus forty degrees and it didn't do me any harm."

"Why didn't you just stay in a hotel?" Joe asked, but she ignored him.

"If he's in the garden all the time, he'll be lonely," Aisling said.

"You can keep him company when you walk him for an hour every day. It'll be good for you and good for him. Now, I don't want to hear another word about it."

Aisling stared out of the window at Hudson. He should be inside. He was part of the family too. It wasn't fair, it just wasn't fair.

"This can't be right," Joe said. He shoved his copy of Mrs Grough's Rules & Regulations under his sister's nose. "Look what time we have to go to bed."

"Seven o'clock?" Aisling spluttered. "I haven't gone to bed at seven since I was a baby."

"It shows," Mrs Grough replied. "Look at your pallid skin, that lank, dry hair. Early to bed will do you the world of good. Now, your parents have given me a room for my stay. I understand that this is a room you may previously have been allowed to access, but while I am here it is my room and not part of your home, much like an embassy in a foreign land. It will remain off limits."

"What?" Joe said. It had been a very long explanation and had confused him.

"Stay out of her room," Aisling said.

"Exactly, stay out of my room. All you two have to do is follow my rules for the next few days and we shall rub along quite well together."

"What happens if we don't want to follow the rules?" Aisling asked.

Mrs Grough smiled a thin-lipped smile. "I wouldn't recommend that. In a battle of wills I'll always come out on top, young lady. I spent almost fourteen years in the army. It was perfect training for a life of self-discipline and success. I do not lose."

★

"This is a disaster. She can't tell us what to do. She's not our mother," Aisling huffed ten minutes later when Mrs Grough was tidying up. They could hear her tut-tutting downstairs as she found a stray sock or more dust or a picture that wasn't hanging perfectly straight.

"All those rules she has are stupid," Aisling continued. "And she can't make Hudson stay outside in the freezing cold all the time. That's just mean."

"It's not really that mean. He does have a heated kennel and a bed that's softer than mine."

"It's mean and she's not going to get away

with it," Aisling said.

"What are you going to do?" Joe asked.

"I don't know yet."

"Let's think about this, Ash. If we just put up with her rules, in four days' time I'll be getting Soccer Blaster X under the Christmas tree. And if you don't cause any trouble, you'll get that Electric Robot Dancer you never stop talking about. Maybe we have to do the right thing for once."

Aisling did want the Electric Robot Dancer. She really did. It had fifty-three different dance functions and played over four thousand songs. She'd wanted it long before everyone else in school wanted one, long before they thought it was cool. She'd hoped to get it

for her birthday in June, but her parents had said it was too expensive, something they said more and more often these days. But there was a chance she'd get it at Christmas. And they did usually try to behave in December so that they could get their presents. Maybe Joe was right. But there was another part of her that didn't want to give in to Mrs Grough, the same part of her that meant she defied all the babysitters who'd come to their home over the last couple of years. Why should she let these strangers order her around? They didn't know her. Only her parents should be allowed to tell her what to do.

"What if we just try one or two little things to show her that we're not wimpy kids and she's not the boss because she's tough and used to be in the army?"

"Yeah, but what if we do something that we think is a tiny little prank but Santa thinks is a big deal and then he decides not to give us our presents? That would be, like, the worst thing that ever happened in the history of the world."

"What's more important to you? Standing up for ourselves or getting some presents?"

"Getting presents. One thousand per cent on getting some presents."

"We'll get presents. Trust me, Joe. Santa's not going to care about some silly little prank. He won't even get to hear about it. It's nearly Christmas Day, so he's too busy to notice. Anyway, you know Victor Loozer, the huge guy in my class?"

"Yes, he took my backpack and threw it on the school roof once, for no reason whatsoever. I liked that backpack, not as much as Mrs Grough seems to like her suitcase, but I still liked it. Victor's nothing but a big jerk."

"Yes, he can be a jerk. Well, he—"

"He's so tough he calls his left fist The

Punisher and his right fist Deathkiller. Who does that? And I heard he once stole a teacher's lunch and ate it right in front of him."

"Yes, I heard that too, but—"

"And he had an arm-wrestling match with the principal and Victor won so the principal had to do all of Victor's homework for the next month."

"Yes, he does all those crazy things and he *still* gets presents from Santa. That's what I'm trying to tell you. Santa's a nice guy, he's not going to ignore us."

"I don't know, Ash. In three days, Mrs Grough will be gone and Mam and Dad will be home and we'll be eating sweets for breakfast and watching films late at night and I'll get Soccer Blaster X. That's all that matters."

Aisling was looking forward to spending time with their parents as well. She didn't think Joe would remember, but back when

Mam and Dad had regular jobs rather than their own business, they'd always spent lots of time together as a family, usually having fun too. Since they'd started their own company, they'd been working like crazy.

"Anyway," Joe continued. "We've not been great this year so I don't know if we should be taking any chances."

"We've not been great? Are you serious? We've been brilliant. Name one time we got into trouble."

"The night we made the waterfall by turning on all the upstairs taps and the garden hose and all that water gushed down the stairs and flooded Mam and Dad's office?"

"Oh yeah, they weren't too happy. But it was a great waterfall," Aisling said.

"The best. And don't forget the night we let those stray goats into the house and they started eating the curtains and Mam's favourite dress and then one of them pooped everywhere."

"We couldn't leave the poor things out on the street like that."

"But there was twelve of them. You know you should never let more than seven goats into a house at any one time," he said. "Oh, and remember the day we turned the kitchen into an indoor skating rink and Dad came in and slid across the floor and smashed into the microwave and broke—"

"OK, OK, I get it," Aisling said.

"I know that look. You're still going to do something, aren't you?"

"Oh yes. Definitely."

✳ Chapter ✳ Four

Mrs Grough had to call them four times before they woke up the first morning. And it was only when she started hoovering right beside his ear that Joe finally dragged himself out of his warm cocoon of a bed.

"I can't manage three days of this," he said to his sister as he stumbled bleary-eyed down the stairs towards a breakfast of watery porridge.

The watery porridge wasn't the worst thing about breakfast. It was Mrs Grough's constant stream of orders that got to Aisling and Joe:

"Take your elbows off the table."

"Sit up straight. Slouching is bad for your posture."

"Don't talk with your mouth full. I don't want to see your insides."

After breakfast they had to wash their bowls and the porridge pot in the kitchen sink. The last of the porridge was stuck fast to the inside of the saucepan.

"This is impossible to clean. We do have a dishwasher, you know, Mrs G," Joe said.

"It's Mrs Grough, never Mrs G. And we have two dishwashers – their names are Aisling and Joe," Mrs Grough replied.

"I think that's supposed to be a joke," Aisling whispered.

"She's hilarious," Joe muttered.

There was a scratching sound at the back

door followed by some whining.

"Hudson!" Aisling said.

She ran to the door and was about to open it when the babysitter stopped her.

"Don't even think about it," she said.

"So what do you do for fun, Mrs Grough?" Joe asked, thinking their babysitter couldn't be this strict and rigid one hundred per cent of the time.

"Fun? I don't see the point of it," she replied.

When she was out of earshot, Joe turned to his sister.

"Maybe one little prank wouldn't be so bad, after all," he said.

It was after lunch when Mrs Grough sat down in Mam's comfy cracked leather armchair to take the fourteen-and-a-half-minute break she'd scheduled in her diary the night before. She hadn't deviated from one of her schedules since late in the summer of 2009 when she was extremely ill and could only manage two hundred and fourteen of her two hundred and fifty daily press-ups.

She was reading a book on the Navy Seals when Aisling and Joe carried in a tray laden down with a delicious assortment of biscuits, a steaming mug of hot chocolate and a bowl of what looked like sugar.

What Mrs Grough didn't know was that Joe had added *a lot* of salt to the bowl so now it was more salt than sugar.

"What's all this?" Mrs Grough asked.

"We made you some hot chocolate," Aisling said.

"We're kind that way," Joe said.

"Self-praise is no praise," Mrs Grough said. "I don't normally indulge my sweet tooth like this."

"You deserve it. You've worked so hard," Joe

said. "And it is Christmas. Everyone's allowed a treat at this time of year."

"As I've already told you, Joseph, Christmas begins on Christmas Day. That's the way it was when I was a girl and there was nothing wrong with it. Now you have Christmas advertisements on television the moment Halloween ends and some people put up their decorations in the middle of November. Utter nonsense and—"

"How many sugars would you like?" Aisling asked, interrupting her rant. "Two? Three?"

"Why not make it four?" Mrs Grough said.

Aisling and Joe glanced at each other and struggled not to laugh. Four spoons of salt? This was going to be brilliant.

Aisling heaped in the sugar-salt, then they stepped back and watched as Mrs Grough took her first sip of the hot chocolate. And then her second. There was no reaction at all. Well, one small reaction – a tiny smile. She looked like she was enjoying it. In no time at all, she'd polished off the entire mug.

"Delicious," she said. "Good idea adding the salt. It goes well with the chocolate. Now, leave me alone. I have ten minutes and forty-five seconds left of my break before I take my afternoon power nap and I'd like to read my book."

The two children stood there with their mouths open. They couldn't believe what they'd just seen. How did she manage to drink that? It must have been disgusting. Still, they weren't going to let one failure to put them off.

Unfortunately for them, their next prank didn't go very well either. Joe had covered up most of the end of the kitchen tap with tape, leaving only a tiny gap for water to emerge.

"Once Mrs G turns on the tap, the water will spray out and soak her," he said. "Then she'll know not to mess with us."

They hid in the living room for ages, hunched down behind the couch, waiting for Mrs Grough to go into the kitchen to start preparing their unappealing soon-to-be-boiled-until-it's-limp-and-soggy dinner. The thought of her shrieking or screaming when she turned on the tap made them giggle in anticipation. They heard her clunk and clatter around the kitchen until, finally, they heard the water gush out of the tap. There wasn't any shrieking or screaming though, and when Mrs Grough left the kitchen a few moments later she was bone dry.

"You must have got it wrong," Aisling said.

"No way. I've done it hundreds of times and it's always worked before," Joe said.

They checked the kitchen tap – the tape was still in place – so Joe turned it on at full force just to test it out. The water sprayed out at wild angles, hitting him directly in the mouth, splashing everywhere from the floor to the top of the fridge and soaking them from head to toe.

"How did she do that? No one's ever got away dry before," Joe gasped. "It's like she's prepared for everything."

"OK, Mrs Grough," Aisling spluttered. "You win this one too, but you can't win them all."

As it turned out, she could win them all. Every last trick they tried over the next few hours failed: the Milk Glue, the Frozen Toothbrush, the Thornberry Twist. Mrs Grough was always one step ahead of them and it wasn't long before Joe had had enough.

"It's time to give up. She's too good for us, Ash. And if we keep going, we'll end up doing something really stupid and spectacular and we'll miss out on Soccer Blaster X and Electric Robot Da—"

"I know, I know," Aisling said, even though

she didn't want to give in. It wasn't in her nature to quit and it just didn't feel right.

Before dinner time, Mrs Grough sat them down at the living-room table.

"It's time we had a little chat because it's become clear that you haven't been paying enough attention to my rules and regulations. I'd hoped it wouldn't come to this because while I am strict, I also like to think of myself as a fair person. But since you have decided to turn this into a battle—"

Joe was worried. In addition to having a nose for trouble, he had an ear for trouble too and he could sense where Mrs Grough's words were heading.

"We don't want a battle. It was just a couple of silly pranks. Cos we're silly. Yep, big old silly stupid-heads. You—"

"Stop, Joseph, you're embarrassing yourself. Now, as I told you before, I always win. I am, after all, an elite babysitter and I have a very particular set of skills, skills I have acquired over a very long career, skills that make me a nightmare for children like you. These foolish pranks are a waste of my time and yours and they've just cost you your internet privileges."

"What?"

"No internet or television for the rest of my stay."

"You can't do that," Aisling said.

"I can and I just have. Do you want further punishment? No? Good. Now take the dog for a walk."

"By ourselves?" Joe asked.

"Yes. I have come up with a route that's safe, but promotes independence for children at the same time."

"I have no idea what you're talking about," Joe said.

"Just take him for a walk," Mrs Grough sighed,

handing Aisling a beautifully hand-drawn map of the neighbourhood, colour-coded and with arrows pointing out the path they should take from start to finish. "And remember, step out of line one more time and there will be trouble. Is that understood?"

"Yes, Mrs Grough," Aisling and Joe said.

They weren't happy about it, but they knew they'd have to follow her rules if they were going to get the Christmas presents they really wanted.

Unfortunately for them, it was the very next day when everything went wrong.

Chapter Five

They were exhausted. Every time Mrs Grough had barked orders, they'd obeyed. They'd hoovered, washed and wiped every surface in the house. They'd cleaned the bathroom tiles with a toothbrush until they were transformed from a drab grey to a sparkling white. They'd tried to put out the rubbish and stifled roars of anguish when the bags had ripped apart and the putrid, disgusting, extra-slimy contents of the bin fell on the kitchen floor, which meant they had to put on gloves and pick it all up piece by rotten piece.

41

"Can we finish now?" Joe asked. He couldn't remember ever having had such a miserable Christmas before.

"Well, you have worked quite hard, so I suppose it's time for you to put your feet up and enjoy the satisfaction of a job well done."

"You really don't understand kids, do you, Mrs Grough?" Joe said.

There was no satisfaction of a job well done, but Aisling and Joe did find that after all that work they were actually hungry enough to wolf down the hairy bacon and pickled sprouts Mrs Grough served up for dinner. And they were so tired that they actually fell asleep at 7.01 p.m. and slept long, dreamless sleeps until the ringing alarm clocks Mrs Grough placed outside their bedroom doors woke them up at 6.30 a.m. in time for their porridge and water.

"I can't stand this. It's like a prison camp," Aisling said. She'd said this approximately four hundred and thirty-seven times in the last twenty-four hours. "And she's so serious all the time. I've never even heard her laugh."

"I thought I saw her smile once, but I think she might just have been trying to stop herself from belching," Joe said.

The situation was made worse by the fact that Hudson still hadn't been allowed into the house. Mrs Grough was a woman of her word and, unlike many other people, when she said something, she really did mean it. Aisling would look at Hudson, his little nose pressed up against the glass, and her heart would almost break. Was he the best-behaved dog in the world? No. Was he likely to cause chaos when he was in the house? Definitely. Did you have to check your shoes for poop every morning before you put them on? Of course. But he was still a member of their family.

It was an hour later when Joe heard the

noise from down the hall. It sounded like it was coming from Mrs Grough's room even though she was downstairs. She'd just finished her workout of two hundred and fifty press-ups and three hundred star jumps and was sitting in the kitchen with a cup of tea and the newspaper. If she wasn't in her room, then who was? he wondered. It took a little while before the answer came to him.

Aisling!

Oh no, he thought. Oh no, oh no, oh no. That wasn't good. That wasn't good at all.

He ran down the hall on tiptoes, trying to be as quiet as possible. He slowly pushed open the bedroom door, grimly determined to prevent it from emitting even a solitary creak.

"What are you doing in there? We're not allowed in her room," he whispered. His sister was on her hands and knees on the spotlessly clean wooden floor, peering under the bed.

"Don't you remember her whole speech about it? It went on for hours, maybe even days."

There was something wrong. Aisling looked worried, really worried. He'd never seen her like this before and he didn't like it.

"Just give me a second," she said.

"No, no. I won't give you a second. If she catches us in here we're dead, as dead as a doodoo."

"Do you mean dodo?" Aisling asked.

"Doodoo, dodo! What difference does it make? We'll be dead," Joe whispered furiously, his eyes bulging. "Get out of here now. I think I hear her. I definitely hear her."

"You don't hear her, you're panicking," said Aisling, who sounded quite anxious herself.

"I'm not panicking, I'm just freaking out. Wait, why are you on your hands and knees? What are you looking for?"

He dropped to the floor and followed her

gaze. Hudson was under the bed, chewing on something. It was quite dark under there and Joe couldn't quite make out what it was.

"Hudson is here? He can't be here. He shouldn't be here. Why did you bring him here?"

"He looked so cold and lonely outside and I . . . well, I missed him being in the house with us, so I snuck him in and instead of staying in my room like he was supposed to he went all Hudson-y and ran in to Mrs Grough's room and—"

"Wait, what's he eating?"

"I'll tell you, but you've got to promise not to make a big deal of it."

There was no need to tell him or for Joe to make any kind of promise. He could see it now. Hudson was chewing on Mrs Grough's suitcase. Or at least what was left of it.

Joe couldn't help himself. He screamed.

Before Aisling had time to shut him up, the scream had alerted Mrs Grough. There was a very brief moment of silence when the world seemed to stop and Aisling thought they just might have got away with it, but then they heard her pounding up the stairs.

Hudson decided that the best time to drag the ripped, half-eaten, drool-covered suitcase from the darkness of under the bed to the harsh light of day was just as Mrs Grough pushed open the bedroom door.

"This will not do," Mrs Grough said through lips both thin and white as she surveyed the scene. "No, this will not do at all."

For Joe, the worst part was that Hudson looked like he was smiling, as if he was proud of what he'd done and expected a treat as a reward. His little tail wagged happily.

⋆ Chapter ⋆ Six

"It was an accident," Joe said.

"An accident?" Mrs Grough said, heading downstairs. "Really? A canine accidentally let himself into the house, then accidentally went into my room, where he accidentally ate my suitcase?"

"He didn't eat *all* of the suitcase," Joe said.

"A suitcase I've had for twenty-six years," Mrs Grough said.

"So it's really old. That's good. We can get you a new one, Mrs Grough. Brand new. Shiny. I have one euro fifty cents. How much

49

is a suitcase? Ten euros? I'll get the rest from somewhere. Have you got any money, Ash?"

They followed Mrs Grough into the kitchen.

"What did I say about the dog?"

"That he isn't allowed in the house. But it was cold and he's small and—" Aisling began.

"What did I say about my room?" she said.

"Not to go in there," Joe said.

"Yes, I told you not to go in there. But you couldn't follow that simple instruction. I warned you yesterday and now you will see that actions have consequences."

"Consequences? What are consequences? Are consequences bad, Ash?"

"They're not good," she said.

Unlike her brother, she had no intention of whining or complaining. Whatever punishment Mrs Grough issued, she'd take it on the chin. Clean the chimney with a Brillo pad? Sweep the snow from the lawn and then cut the grass with nail clippers? Scrub the toilet with a toothbrush? She'd do whatever she was told and Mrs Grough wouldn't hear a single peep from her. She'd show her that she was just as tough as someone who was in the army.

"What's she doing?" Joe whispered to his sister.

Mrs Grough sat at the kitchen table and took an old-fashioned luxury writing set from her handbag. She paused for a moment, thinking about what she wanted to say, before writing for over a minute. Then, satisfied with what she'd written, she folded the letter in two and placed it in a crisp white envelope. She stuck a stamp in the upper-right corner before writing the address.

Joe couldn't believe his eyes.

"Oh no," he said. "No, no, no, no, no. This is bad, this is very, very bad."

Aisling had to nudge her brother out of the

way to see what Mrs Grough had written. It was a two-line address, both clear and simple:

SANTA
NORTH POLE

Aisling felt her stomach plunge to her toes. She thought she was going to be sick. This was a joke, wasn't it? Mrs Grough wouldn't dare.

Their babysitter stood up, put on her coat and shoes, crooked her handbag over her arm and left the house without another word.

"Is she?" Joe said.

"She is," Aisling replied.

They raced after her. She was moving quickly, striding forwards with her chin in the air and a sense of purpose in her feet. Aisling and Joe ran down the snowy street until they'd caught up with her.

"I presume you're wondering what's in

the letter," Mrs Grough said, without even glancing at them as they hopped and danced around her. "It's quite simple. I've told Mr Claus how awful you've been. I suggested to him that you should not be on the good list this year."

"Nooooooo," Joe cried. "If we're on the bad list we won't get any presents. You don't understand what you're doing, Mrs Grough; you're ruining Christmas."

"On the contrary, I know exactly what I'm doing, Joseph."

The street was becoming busier as Christmas shoppers rushed around doing their next-to-last-minute business. Those who had already finished all their shopping and were feeling quite smug about it stopped to gaze at the developing drama.

"It was one little mistake. One teeny, tiny little mistake," Joe said.

"You allowed the dog indoors. You went

into my room. You failed to tell me about any of it."

"Three little mistakes."

"And the pranks?"

"Five little mistakes. Maybe six. But no more than seven."

"It wasn't Joe's fault, it was mine. I let Hudson in. I went into your room. Don't punish Joe," Aisling said.

"Yes, don't punish me, punish Aisling," Joe cried.

"You were both in the room, therefore I hold both of you responsible."

"We'll be good, we'll do whatever you want," Joe said. "For the next ten years."

That was too long, wasn't it?

"Well, not ten years, but for the next year. We'll make your dinner."

What do adults like? Think, Joe, think. Boring stuff. That's it, adults like boring stuff.

"We'll change duvet covers and we'll talk about how much a litre of milk costs and, and—"

They had reached a postbox. Mrs Grough stopped and looked them both in the eye.

"I can see you're being sincere and I do appreciate that," she said. "But you also seem to believe you can talk your way out of anything. Sometimes the lessons that benefit us the most in life are the toughest ones to learn. You'll thank me for this in twenty years' time."

"When I'm thirty-nine? Santa's not going to visit me when I'm ancient."

Mrs Grough rolled her eyes. Poor mathematical skills – yet another problem with modern children, she thought.

"I'll wash your car – oh, wait, you walked here. I'll polish your shoes and they'll shine so much you'll see your face in them. So shiny you'll even see all your wrinkles. And ... and ... you like manners and stuff – I'll give

Auntie Dee a kiss on the cheek every time I meet her," Joe said.

He hated kissing his Auntie Dee more than he hated anything in the world, so that would be a huge sacrifice, but even that wasn't enough to stop Mrs Grough.

"Please don't do it, Mrs G. Please," Joe said.

Without another word, she popped the letter into the postbox.

⋆ Chapter ⋆ Seven

Aisling was more upset than she'd ever been before in her life, but she wasn't about to let Mrs Grough see that. She held her chin up high, and even though tears welled up in the corners of her eyes, she refused to let them fall.

Joe's reaction was a little less dignified. He launched himself at the postbox, his right arm extended like a superhero taking off. His hand shot right into the mail slot, all the way in until he was up to his shoulder in the mailbox.

"Yeah, this was a huge mistake," he said moments later. "I can't find the letter and my arm's stuck."

Mrs Grough tut-tutted. "Don't you have any pride, boy?"

"I think it's quite clear that I don't," Joe said, although he was growing a little embarrassed now that passers-by had started laughing and pointing at him. A girl from his class gave him a supportive thumbs up before taking a photo of him with her phone.

"Free yourself immediately and then follow me home," Mrs Grough said, turning on her heel and striding off.

Luckily, a postman arrived less than a minute later, and with his help – and some cooking oil and butter from a nearby shop to loosen Joe's arm – Joe, much to his relief, was soon free, even if his jacket did smell quite bad afterwards.

"You're an extremely enthusiastic letter poster. I like that, especially since most young people don't care about letters any more. It's all tablets and phones and electronic biddlybobs these days," the postman said. "What's the problem? Last-minute letter to Santa?"

"Yes, we forgot to send our letter to Santa until today and we wrote it so quickly we never asked ..." Aisling began. An idea popped into her head. "... we never asked him for presents for our parents. They're great parents and we really, really wanted to get some presents for them. We love them soooo much."

"Huh?" Joe said. Then he caught on. "Oh yeah, right. It's not like we want anything for ourselves, it's for everyone else."

"Isn't that lovely. You're such thoughtful children," the postman said.

He took out a key and opened the door of the postbox.

"That's me, thoughtful, thoughtful, thoughtful," Joe said. "My dad always says: *You spend too much time thinking about other people, Joe. You should really be more selfish.* And I say—"

Aisling elbowed him in the ribs and made a face at him to let him know he was laying it on too thick. The postman began scooping the letters from the postbox into a large brown mailbag. Aisling's heart jumped when she spotted the letter with Mrs Grough's perfectly neat handwriting at the top of one of the piles of last-minute Christmas cards.

"There it is," she cried, pointing to it. "Can we have our letter back so we can change it?"

The postman's beaming face suddenly transformed into one that was much more serious.

"You want your letter back? Oh no, young lady. Absolutely not. Once the letter goes into the postbox it cannot be retrieved. It absolutely, positively must go to the address on the envelope. That's the law. Us postal workers take our jobs very seriously indeed."

"But it's right there. I can see it. I could just go and pick—"

"I said no and I mean no," the postman said,

closing the bag with an unnecessary flourish. "Now, if you want to write another letter to the great man, I'm sure he'd be more than happy to read it."

"Of course, that's it, we'll write another letter to cancel out Mrs G's letter!" Joe whispered to his sister. "We'll tell Santa that she only sent it as a joke and that—"

"Although," the postman said, rubbing his chin, "now that I think of it, this is the last lot of post that will reach its destination before Christmas. If you post your letter later today he should get it by the twenty-seventh of December, maybe the twenty-eighth."

"But that's too late. It's Christmas Day in less than two days."

"Yes, it is, isn't it? Sorry about that," the postman said before slinging the postbag over his shoulder and walking off, whistling cheerfully.

The children trudged back home, not even enjoying the crunch of snow beneath their feet.

"Is this really happening or is it a nightmare?" Joe said. "She's actually written to Santa telling him that we've been bad. I can't believe it. You hear rumours about people doing things like that, and I know parents threaten it all the time – *If you don't behave, I'll write to Santa and you won't get any presents* – but you never think it's really going to happen. Except this time it actually has."

He was feeling thoroughly sorry for himself, but Aisling's brain was whirring at a million miles a second.

"This isn't over yet," she said. "It's just one letter. All we have to do is find some way to make sure that Santa knows that we should get our presents."

"Do you think that would work?" Joe asked, brightening a little at the idea that not all hope was lost.

"Definitely. We've never been on the list before. Once Santa knows that the whole thing is a big mistake then everything will be fine."

"OK, that's good. How can we get in touch with him? Think, Joe, think. I've got it – why don't we email him? Does Santa have an email address? What do you think it is?" Joe asked.

"Doesn't matter. We don't have any internet, remember? Mrs Grough banned it. And we can't get to Mam and Dad's computer. It's in their office and the office is locked."

"We could pick the lock."

"Do you know how to pick a lock?"

"No, but I could figure out how to do it. I'm very clever."

"You just got your arm stuck in a postbox."

"Oh yeah, that's true. Maybe I'm not that clever after all."

"Is there still some of that red paint in the garage?" Aisling asked.

"Plenty. Only half the tin spilled on Mrs Doyle's head that time, the rest is still OK. Why?"

"I've got another idea."

By the time they arrived back home, Mrs Grough had embarked on her afternoon army exercises. Even though she was almost three quarters of the way through them, she'd barely broken a sweat. Because she followed exactly the same routine every day, Aisling and Joe knew that she'd soon be sitting in Mam's armchair reading a book and when she'd finished reading she'd take her half-hour afternoon power nap. That would give them the free time they needed.

Chapter Eight

While Mrs Grough gently snored, tired from her exercises, Aisling, Joe and Hudson were in the garage. It was much colder than in the house so they could see their breath, little puffs of white billowing out ahead of them. Joe was on his knees on the concrete floor in front of a large white bedsheet he'd taken from the hot press. He had used the last of the red paint to write some large letters on the sheet. They read:

SANTA –
PLEASE LAND HERE
AND GIVE US LOADS
OF PRESENTS. IGNOOR
LETTER FROM MRS G.
WE'VE BEN GOOD.

"*Ignoor*? We've *ben* good. Your spelling's terrible," Aisling said. "But it'll have to do."

She began to dry the paint with her small yellow hairdryer, hoping the whooshing sound it made wouldn't wake Mrs Grough up.

"I don't really understand how this is going to work," Joe said.

Aisling switched off the hairdryer. "Tomorrow's Christmas Eve. We'll tie this sheet to the roof of the house and when Santa flies over in his sleigh, he'll see the message and realize he should give us our presents."

"You're a genius," Joe said. "Will we put it on the roof now?"

"No, Mrs Grough will see it and take it down. We'll put it up at the last minute. But maybe we should practise now so it'll be perfect when we do it tomorrow night."

"You think of everything, Ash," Joe chirped.

They set to work, so excited by the prospect of their plan coming together that they forgot to put on their gloves. Soon their hands were icy cold, but they didn't care. While Hudson supervised, they tied a piece of blue rope to each corner of the bedsheet, then carried it out into the back garden.

"Bit windy," Joe said as the sheet flapped up in front of him. It had been snowing earlier, but now it had clouded over and the wind had picked up. Some of the reindeers and cheery Santa decorations in their neighbours' gardens began to rattle and shake.

"Yip," Hudson barked, warning the wind to keep away.

They looked up at the roof. It was high and the ice-and-snow-covered tiles appeared slippy and dangerous. The thought of climbing all the way up there made them nervous. But Aisling wasn't about to let fear stop her.

"We'll need a ladder," she said.

"I'll get one," Joe replied, dropping the bedsheet and running towards the garage.

A yelp from Hudson made him stop. The wind had gusted and caught the sheet lifting it into the air. Aisling hung on to the blue rope as the weather threatened to steal their hard work away.

"Don't just stand there, Joe. Help me," she said.

Joe ran back and grabbed another strand of rope just in time as the sheet flapped and whip-cracked around the garden, dragging them left and right, their feet furrowing the snow as they clung on grimly. Hudson decided it was time to help and leaped up, grabbing a third piece of rope between his teeth.

"Good boy," Aisling said. "You're a brilliant dog."

"Hmmmmppph," Hudson agreed.

"That was close," Joe said, "but we've got it under control now."

He was wrong. Without any warning, the bedsheet took off like a kite-rocket, blasted into the winter sky by a huge gust. And it carried one dog and two children high into the air. Within seconds they were flying over the snow-covered rooftops and streets of the town.

"Don't let go," Aisling shouted as they were buffeted around.

"What makes you think we'd let go?" Joe shouted back. "We're not idiots."

"Rrrrrghhhhh," Hudson affirmed.

Down on the street below, they spotted a neighbour taking his grocery shopping from the boot of his car.

"Hello, Mr Quigley," Joe shouted.

The man looked up – lost in thought, wondering if he should have bought an extra jar of cranberry sauce just to be on the safe side – and absent-mindedly smiled and waved.

"Oh, hi, Joe, hello there, Aisling. And is that little Hudson I see too?" he said. "Happy Christmas to you and your family."

Then it dawned on him that seeing flying children and dogs in the sky was not a normal thing and he began to panic. He jumped up and down as if he didn't know what else to do.

"Help, help. Look. There in the sky," he shouted to the passers-by. "My neighbours are flying either on a bedsheet adorned with some crudely rendered red lettering or else a kind of out-of-control magic carpet. Call the gardaí,

72

call the army, call the airport, call someone!"

By the time anyone else had looked up, another gust had whisked them past the church and out of sight, which left Mr Quigley feeling confused and wondering if his eyes had been deceiving him.

Twenty metres up in the air, they swirled and swooped, completely out of control, their hair flying wildly, their arms aching as they clung on to the ropes for dear life. Only Hudson appeared to be enjoying it.

Everything appeared distant and weird when seen from this strange new point of view. They noticed Frisbees and other toys stuck on roofs, houses with perfectly neat front gardens and perfectly messy back gardens. They spotted a group of children around Aisling's age sliding down Tuckey's Hill using shiny plastic coal bags as makeshift toboggans. They came face to beak with a plump seagull who was astonished to find humans in the air and had to peck himself to make sure he wasn't dreaming.

On and on they flew, past the town centre and out towards the housing estates and flats on its edges. Eventually, the wind began to die down.

"We're going to land. We have to guide ourselves carefully if we don't want to crash into a building," Aisling roared.

As the gusts and blusters gradually eased to a soft breeze, they began to float towards an estate where the houses were much smaller than their home and everything

appeared to have been squashed together.
There were decorations in most of the front
gardens and cheerful polar bears, snowmen
and penguins in the windows. Many houses

had wreaths on the front door and twinkling lights strung along the edge of the roof. But there were two houses side by side, nestled in a corner of the estate, that stood apart from all the others. These houses were free from all Christmas cheer and bleaker than the rest. And it was one of these houses, the grim-looking last house on the left, that they were heading towards.

On the far side of the houses lay a small woodland with winter-bare trees. Just beyond that were the white-covered fields and hills where the town ended and the countryside began, but Aisling didn't think they'd be able to make it that far.

"If we get higher we can just about make those woods," she shouted.

They looked like they'd make for a softer and safer landing than the roof of someone's house. Joe pursed his lips and started blowing air at the bedsheet to make it rise higher. To his surprise that didn't work at all.

They were ten metres up in the air and twenty metres from the house when its front door opened and a large boy, with hair that could only be described as angry, emerged. Aisling and Joe recognized him at once. It was Victor Loozer, the toughest kid in school, the kid who was supposed to have named his fists Deathkiller and The Punisher.

Chapter Nine

"**W**e're not going to make the woods," Joe cried. He was right; they were descending at too fast a pace now. "And we can't land on his house. He'll squash us like bugs. Abort the mission, abort the mission."

If Victor was surprised at seeing two children and a dog appear overhead, he didn't show it. He was too cool for that.

"Lean right, lean right," Aisling said as the ground hurtled towards them at a dizzying speed, a great rush of footpaths and concrete walls and red-nosed reindeer decorations.

"Hudson can't tell left from right," Joe squeaked, unsure if he fully knew the difference himself.

But either through luck or the secret genius of their dog, at the very last moment they managed to steer just enough to swing away from Victor's raggedy front garden and instead ploughed right into the house next door.

Joe smashed into the window as Aisling bounced off the pebble-dash wall, while Hudson released the rope just in time to make a perfect four-pawed landing right in the centre of the rubbish-strewn garden.

"What the—" Joe began as his nose conked off the double-glazed glass.

Staring out of the window was a sea of cats. At least ten, maybe even twelve. Cats of different sizes and colours, some large and luxuriantly coated, others small and fluffy.

They were lined up in a row on the inside windowsill, looking at the trespassers in their garden.

Joe and Aisling had barely got to their feet when the front door swung open and a furious old man, in a dressing gown and slippers, slid down the icy steps, swinging his walking stick around his head like a samurai sword.

"Burglars, thieves, trespassers, varmints, stinky good-for-nothings," he shouted. "Get out of my garden."

From inside the house came what sounded like a thousand miaows. Aisling and Joe didn't have time to do anything other than run. They hopped over the small front wall, Hudson leading the way.

"The bedsheet!" Aisling cried.

"Leave it!" Joe yelped as the old man shuffled after them.

"If I see you around here again, there'll

be trouble," he shouted before turning to his neighbour. "What are you looking at, boy? Don't you dare even glance in my direction."

Victor rolled his eyes but didn't say anything. The man swung his walking stick around his head once more before disappearing indoors.

Victor managed to move in front of Aisling and Joe before they could escape.

"Hey, melon heads. Where do you think you're going?"

They stopped immediately. There was something about his voice and presence that made them freeze.

"Please don't hurt me," Joe said, squeezing his eyes shut in anticipation of a punch.

Aisling elbowed him to be quiet.

"Oh, hello, Victor. Didn't see you there," she said.

"How do you know my name?" Victor asked, his eyes narrowing like a predator

eyeing up its prey.

"We're in the same class in school."

"Oh yeah. Thought you looked familiar. You're that rich girl."

Rich? Aisling didn't think she was rich. Her parents were always worrying about money.

"What are you doing around here?" he asked.

The last thing Aisling wanted was to embarrass herself by telling him the truth, so she decided to lie instead.

"We made our own parachute and since it was windy today we thought we'd try it out. Boy, did that go wrong. Flying through the air like that. Crazy stuff. Your neighbour wasn't too happy when we landed in his garden."

"Mr Grindle? He's always angry. He hates everyone and everything. Dogs. Kids. Apples. Cups. Snow globes. Cows. Lawns. Balloons. Tyres. Christmas. Everything. You name it, he hates it. He's only happy when he's got something to complain about."

"He might hate everything, but he sure likes cats," Joe said.

"Only visitors he ever has is cats," Victor said, before swiftly changing the subject. "Why did your sister lie to me?"

"L–l–lie?" Joe stuttered. "She didn't lie. She never lies. Why would she lie? Did she lie? I'm so sorry she lied. Please forgive me."

"I'm not stupid. I can read, you know," Victor said. "I saw what was written on your useless parachute. Your message to Santa. Why would you write something like that on a sheet unless you were in trouble? Is Santa really not going to call at your house tomorrow night? Why not? What did you do? It must have been really bad."

Aisling stood there defiantly, her arms folded. "It's none of your business what we did or didn't do," she said.

Joe's face turned white. Was his sister really standing up to Victor? What was wrong with her? Aisling stared at Victor and Victor stared at Aisling. Neither of them moving, neither of them giving in, even as they both began to shiver from the cold.

"This is getting weird now," Joe said.

And then Aisling had an idea. Possibly a terrible idea, but an idea nonetheless.

"Victor, can I ask you something?" she said, breaking the silence between them.

"Please don't," Joe said. "Let's go home before he crushes us or—" He noticed Victor was glaring at him. "Did I say crushes? I meant . . . I don't know what I meant. Me not so good with words."

"Be quiet, Joe. Just listen to me, Victor. Five minutes, that's all I need."

To Joe's surprise, the big bruiser nodded in agreement. To his even bigger surprise, Aisling told Victor what had happened, how Mrs Grough had come to stay, her rules and regulations and how she had written to Santa and ruined their Christmas. And Victor didn't shout at them or laugh at them or punch them. Instead, he listened carefully to every word she said.

"Why are you telling me this?" he asked when she finished her story.

"You do things that get you in trouble,

don't you?"

"S'pose so," Victor said.

"But in school you always boas— talk about the brilliant Christmas presents you get. That means you must know how to get back on Santa's good list."

"So what?"

"We want you to help us."

"We do?" Joe said. He didn't want to spend a second longer in Victor's company. He wanted to go home right now. Surely, it was only a matter of time until Victor remembered that he should be performing some kind of violent act, possibly Christmas-themed, like squashing him down a chimney or being inventive with a piece of holly.

"Why should I help you? You never talk to me in school and suddenly you want my help?"

That's true, Aisling thought, she didn't talk to him in school, but that wasn't unusual. As far as she knew, nobody ever spoke to Victor unless, of course, they were begging for mercy. But now she needed his help, she really did. She gave the matter some thought.

"I'm not asking you to be nice or help us because you like us or anything as ridiculous as that. If you do this for us . . . then we'll give you some of our Christmas presents."

Joe gasped.

"Stop being so dramatic, Joe," Aisling sighed.

Which presents was she going to give him? And, more importantly, whose presents?

"I don't want your presents," Victor said, much to Joe's relief. "But if I help you, you'll owe me a favour."

"What does that mean?" Joe asked.

"It means that we'll have to do something for Victor in the future."

Joe didn't like the sound of that at all. What

if he asked them to do something dangerous or scary? Not silly stuff like pranks on babysitters, but something Victor-like, dangerous or scary. No way, that was definitely not going to happen.

"OK, we agree," Aisling said.

Joe was too shocked to speak.

"Good. Come into my house and we'll get started," Victor said.

"We can't. We have to get home before Mrs Grough wakes up. Can you call at our house in about forty minutes?"

"I can do whatever I want whenever I want, cos I'm the coolest kid in town," Victor said.

"Is that a yes?"

"Yes."

Aisling and Joe set off for home, stomping along the snowy footpaths, trying desperately to warm up. Joe waited until Victor was well out of earshot before he said anything, then after checking over his shoulder three times, just to be sure, he spoke.

"Are you crazy?" he asked.

"What?"

"We owe Victor a favour! What if the favour is something like helping him in a fight or something? I could be mangled. I'm too handsome to be mangled."

"That won't happ—"

"And that's not the worst thing. The worst thing is you've just invited the scariest kid in town to our home. You gave him our address. He knows where we live. He knows where we live! It was OK when we only had to worry about him when we were in school, but now he could call any time. We'll have to keep our eyes open twenty-six hours a day."

"I'm sure it'll be fine," Aisling said, although she didn't sound too convinced. "Would you prefer not to get any presents? Because that's

90

the only other option."

"Can't play with my presents if I'm dead, Ash. That's all I'm saying."

Chapter Ten

The walk back to their house took them almost half an hour. They were cold and damp, but for once they had a lucky break. Mrs Grough had slept longer than she usually did – which meant she was grumpy, as her schedule was now off by eleven minutes – and Aisling and Joe were delighted to find that she'd only woken up when she'd heard their voices in the kitchen.

After such a cold and stressful afternoon, they would have loved nothing more than to sit in front of a roaring fire with hot chocolate – topped with mini marshmallows – and brownies fresh from the oven with a dollop of cream on the side. Instead, they were given out to by Mrs Grough for not taking their shoes off before entering the house. They had to dry the snow they'd dragged in from outside before they were each given an ice-cold glass of milk and an apple.

"There's nothing as Christmassy as an apple," Joe said gloomily.

"There's a strange, wild-haired boy outside," Mrs Grough said, peering out of the kitchen window shortly after.

Joe's heart began to thump wildly. Victor was here. And it was Mrs Grough who'd alerted them to his presence, not Hudson. Some guard dog he was. The toughest child in school arrives at their door and what does Hudson do? Joe glanced out of the window and saw exactly what Hudson was doing, which was wagging his tail and letting Victor pet him.

Mrs Grough opened the back door.

"Good afternoon, your ladyship," Victor said. He licked the palm of his hand and slicked his hair back from his forehead. "I'm Victor, a friend of Aisling and Jimmy."

"Who's Jimmy?" Mrs Grough asked.

Victor looked confused. Was he at the wrong house?

"That's me. Jimmy's my nickname," Joe said, appearing at her side, and just about managing to cover up Victor's blunder.

"Your nickname is Jimmy? What's wrong with children these days? Even their nicknames are terribly unimaginative. My three best friends in the army were Scuttles McGinty, Angry Bear and The Steamroller. Now they're proper nicknames."

"That's a great story," Victor said. "Anyhoo, I'm here to help Aisling and Jimmy Joe take the dog for a walk."

Hudson wagged his tail even more

vigorously at the mention of the word walk. First flying, then a new friend, now a walk. This was shaping up to be the best day ever.

"It takes three of you to walk one dog? Well, isn't that just typical. Fine, off you go, but stick to the planned route and make sure you're back here in an hour."

They put on their puffy winter jackets – Aisling's was fur-lined – scarves, and remembered their gloves this time, before heading off. As they walked towards the centre of town – Hudson's good humour spoiled a little by having to wear a leash – Victor practised his evil stare, something he did regularly just to keep in tip-top tough-kid shape. It worked, judging by the number of children who were crossing to the other side of the street to get away from him. One or two looked a bit surprised to see Aisling and Joe with him, but none of them were brave enough to say a word about it.

"What's the plan?" Joe asked.

"You'll see," Victor said. "Follow me and keep up cos I move quick."

They passed by Wonderwink's Toyshop. The window was filled with decorations, from silver garlands to lanterns with a warm glow to thick-knit stockings pinned above a fireplace. Piles of books and board games and puzzles sat on an old-fashioned sledge. A wooden German nutcracker was offering a luxury chocolate to a Scandinavian Christmas gnome. A large teddy bear wearing a Santa hat was behind the wheel of an electric car, his passenger a cuddly, pleasant-looking fox. It all reminded them – as if they needed reminding – that unless they did something quickly they would be spending Christmas without any presents.

Finally, they made their way through the bustling crowds and out-of-tune carollers and found themselves outside a travel agency.

"What is this place?"

"This is a shop where old people who can't figure out how to work the internet go to buy their holidays," Victor said.

"We're going on holiday?" Joe asked.

"We're going to get a plane to the North Pole and when we get there we're going to explain to Santa that you shouldn't be on the list. He'll understand and then everything will be all right," Victor said as he marched confidently through the door.

"We're closing," said Mr Seamus Barry, the man behind the counter, as the three children and Hudson bundled their way into his travel agency. "And canines are not allowed in this establishment."

Joe looked confused.

"He means Hudson," Aisling said.

Seamus Barry was a small, neat man. A

triangle of white handkerchief peeped out from the breast pocket of his dark suit. Everything in his office was just so.

"We want three tickets to the North Pole," Victor said when Joe and Hudson had gone outside.

Mr Barry took the handkerchief from his pocket, covered his mouth with it and laughed precisely three times. It wasn't a hearty laugh. A sniggering squirrel would have made more noise.

"Three tickets to the North Pole?" he spluttered through the white material. He tapped some keys on his computer, checked the screen, then turned to them again. "Do you have two thousand seven hundred and thirty-five euros?"

"No," Victor said.

"How much money do you have?"

They checked their pockets, went outside

to see how much money Joe had, then added everything up.

"We have four euros and twenty-nine cents," Aisling said.

"And a two-euro burger voucher," Victor added.

"Then it seems you cannot afford the flights," said Mr Barry.

He was taken aback when he saw the crestfallen looks on their faces and allowed himself an extremely brief moment of sympathy before

returning to his precise and logical manner.

"May I ask why you want to travel to the North Pole?"

"Me and Santa have some business to discuss," Victor said glumly.

"Have you indeed? Well, if you wish to have a conversation with Mr Claus it might be easier to visit him in Hanrahan's than to travel all the way to the North Pole," Mr Barry said.

VISIT MALLOW

Hanrahan's was the town's largest department store.

"But he's not there now, is he? He's far too busy. Tomorrow's Christmas Eve," Aisling said, her voice trembling with hope and excitement. Maybe they had one last chance after all.

"Well, I do think the great man works too hard, but he is there until six p.m., maybe even five past six, as Hanrahan's are often quite slovenly when it comes to timekeeping. Now, please leave my shop. It is five p.m. and I am not going to be late closing for the first time in thirty-three years because of some children with four euros and twenty-nine cents."

"And a two-euro burger voucher," Victor said as they pushed at the door marked "pull".

Mr Barry sighed and ushered them out of the way before pulling the door open.

"He's in Hanrahan's!" Aisling cried as she raced past Joe and Hudson.

"Who?"

"Who? Santa Claus, of course. We'll get him to change his mind even if it means us having to be good for a whole month."

Hanrahan's was in the shopping centre on the far side of town.

"We'll have to be quick," Victor said.

Chapter Eleven

They took off, slipping and sliding and running and racing along the crowded streets. Through a swell of people laden down with bags of shopping and armfuls of presents. Hudson's leash kept tangling around people's legs and Joe had to stop at least three times to untangle it. Not everybody took the entangling in good Christmas spirit and there were some mutterings and grumblings and stern complaints. By the time they reached the shopping centre they were hot and clammy and out of breath. But most importantly of all, they'd made it in time.

Santa's grotto was at the back of Hanrahan's. It was a welcoming winter wonderland with an arch covered with Christmas lights and a winding little path that led to Santa's hut. There were only two people in the queue ahead of them. They lined up impatiently.

"This is going to work. I just know it," Aisling said. She was beaming from ear to ear. "Thanks for helping us, Victor."

Victor wasn't used to being thanked and found to his surprise that he liked it.

An elf approached them. He was dressed in cheerful greens and reds, with a fluffy white bobble at the end of his long hat, but he didn't look best pleased to see them.

"More visitors?" he sighed. "Leaving it to the last minute, aren't you?"

"Sorry, we—"

"More work for Jiggles. Brilliant."

"Are you . . . Jiggles?" Joe asked.

"Yeah, Jiggles the Elf. You got a problem with that?"

All three of them shook their heads.

The small queue moved slowly and Aisling kept checking her watch, worried that the grotto would close before they got to meet Santa.

"Do you fly to the North Pole every year?" Joe asked Victor when the silence between them had become unbearably uncomfortable.

"What? No, I've never gone there. Why?"

"Because that's what you were going to do with us – fly to the North Pole and persuade Santa that we'd been good. Why were we doing that if you've never done it before?"

"Oh yeah, no, I was doing that because your babysitter put you on the list. That's never happened to me. Nobody ever wrote to Santa to put me on the list," Victor said.

"What? Is that true?" Aisling asked.

She'd assumed Victor had been on the list

lots of times, because, well, you know, because of all the Victor stuff that he did.

"Yeah, never been on the list, but don't worry about it. Santa's cool. Once we explain it to him, he'll understand and you'll be back in the good books again. Just relax, there's nothing to worry about."

"Easy for you to say," Joe said.

"Gnnnnrrrhh," Hudson agreed.

Finally, it was their turn to meet Santa Claus. A young girl emerged from the other side of the grotto carrying a small present. She looked thrilled to have met Santa. She waved a cheery goodbye to Jiggles, who rolled his eyes in reply.

"Your turn," said the elf. "Got your five euros ready?"

They'd forgotten they'd have to pay.

"We've got four euros and twenty-nine cents," said Joe.

"And a two-euro burger voucher," Victor piped up.

"Oh, I appear to have made a terrible mistake. I must have accidentally said the price is four euros and twenty-nine cents and a two-euro burger voucher when I meant to say the price is five euros. I do apologize," Jiggles said.

"No, you did say five euros, it's just that we—" Aisling began. "Wait, you weren't being serious, were you?"

"What gave it away? It's five euros per person," said Jiggles. "And no dogs allowed."

"You see, we left the house in a rush and we didn't realize we'd need money and—"

"Sounds like a great story. Why don't you email the rest of it to jiggles@dontcare.com?"

They searched every pocket in their trousers, in their coats, in their shirts, once, twice and finally for a third time. They even checked their socks just in case. When that was no good, they looked around the floor of the shopping centre hoping to find a coin someone else had dropped, but, of course, just because they needed it so badly, there was none there.

"I'm closing up unless you've got the money."

"We don't have the money, but we have to see Santa. It's an emergency," Joe wailed.

"I'm sure it is. But it's also five euros."

"Can't you just let us in, please? Just this once. It's Christmas," Aisling said as politely as she could even though her temper was rising.

"Sure, I can let you in," said the elf. "If you've got five euros."

"But we just want to—" Joe began as Aisling suddenly realized Victor was nowhere to be seen. He'd disappeared.

"*You* just want to?" Jiggles continued. "Why is it always what *you* want? What about what Jiggles wants? Do you think I enjoy standing here all day? My feet hurt, my back aches, one kid was sick all over me and I mean *all* over me. Some nasty children brought snow in from outside just to make snowballs and throw them at me. What kind of person does that? And if I hear one more *elf and safety* joke my head will explode. Being an elf is supposed to be magical, but not when you're stuck at the back of a shopping centre. You know who's magical? Those North Pole elves. They've got it made, I tell you, with their toys and songs and candy canes."

It was quite the rant, but Aisling had worries of her own.

"I think you must be the grumpiest elf I've ever met," she said.

"Really? How many elves have you actually met?"

Before she had the chance to answer, Victor raced past at top speed, his hands slicing through the air, his legs pumping like pistons, sprinting as if he was being pursued by a pack of wolves or a bear or a yeti, even though there was no one behind him.

Jiggles didn't even seem to notice. "And nobody cares that I'm the only elf that's never got to ride on Santa's sleigh. We've all got our problems, kids."

He shut the gate just as the store announcer said to leave the shop as it was now closing. It was all over. They had failed.

Chapter Twelve

There was no sign of Victor when they left the shopping centre. It was as if once he'd started running he was moving at such speed he couldn't stop. Joe reckoned that if he continued at his current pace he'd probably reach the Atlantic Ocean by midnight.

"He's probably one of those people who are too rude to say goodbye. I never liked him anyway," Joe said.

"He was trying to help us."

"Oh yeah, maybe he wasn't so bad then. But

it doesn't matter, does it? We're still not getting any presents from Santa this year. None. N-U-N, none."

"It's not too late yet," Aisling said.

"Have you got another plan?"

"No," she admitted.

"Well, then it is too late."

They trudged home in gloomy silence. Aisling wracked her brains to come up with some kind of idea, but she couldn't think of anything. Tomorrow was Christmas Eve. It used to be her favourite day of the year, a day when their parents weren't working for once and they all sat around together like one of those perfect families you'd see on television, playing board games and eating boxes of chocolates. Of course, their family wasn't perfect – she'd bicker with Joe, Mam would moan that the fire was too hot and Dad always complained when he'd get to the second layer of the box of chocolates only to find that Joe had snuck in there already and eaten his favourites. But she'd still loved it. Now, she wouldn't be seeing Mam and Dad until late at night and then Christmas Day would follow and what would they get from Santa? A big, fat nothing.

They had just finished a thoroughly unpleasant dinner when it was time for bed. Seven o'clock, lights out. They lay in their beds wide awake for the next couple of hours.

Joe was just about to continue feeling extremely sorry for himself when he heard a *clink, clinkety clink* at the windowpane. He crept out of bed and slowly opened the window to find Aisling was leaning out of her bedroom window too. At the back of the house, Hudson by his side, was Victor. He had been throwing pebbles at their windows. When he saw them he gestured at them to

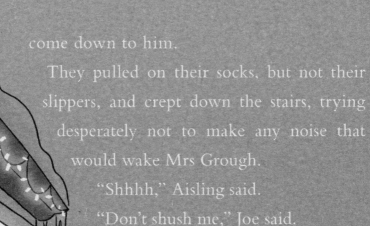

come down to him.

They pulled on their socks, but not their slippers, and crept down the stairs, trying desperately not to make any noise that would wake Mrs Grough.

"Shhhh," Aisling said.

"Don't shush me," Joe said.

"Stop talking. She'll hear us."

"It's your fault I'm talking. If you hadn't shushed me I wouldn't have said anything."

"Shhhh."

They opened the back door and found Victor standing there. He looked surprised when he saw them.

"Why are you in your pyjamas? And why is your house so dark? It's only nine o'clock," he said.

"Shhhh, be quiet," Aisling said. "We don't want to wake Mrs Grough or we'll get in trouble."

"Worse trouble than not getting any Christmas presents?"

He has a point, she thought. How could things get any worse? She ushered him into the kitchen.

"I'm starving," he said. "Got any sweets?"

"Mrs G has hidden all the sweets. We've got plenty of apples and oatcakes, though," Joe said.

"I'm not *that* hungry. I'll get some chips later," Victor said. "Big Sam fan, huh?"

Joe realized, to his horror, that he was wearing Fireman Sam pyjamas. His cheeks flushed immediately. He'd be a laughing stock in school if word got out that he was still a member of Team Sam at his age. But Victor didn't seem to care. He was teasing him in a good-natured way. He seemed happy and not as intimidating as he usually was. That was odd.

"I don't mean to be rude, but why are you here?" Aisling asked. "And why did you run away from the grotto?"

Victor beamed. "You two are going to be so impressed with me."

"Just tell us."

"When Giggles—"

"Jiggles."

". . . said we couldn't get to see Santa, I wasn't just going to sit there crying and sulking about it like Jimmy Joe here," he began.

"I wasn't crying, I was—"

"Be quiet, Jimmy Joe," Aisling said.

"So I came up with another plan. I thought to myself, you know, there's millions and billions and trillions of kids in the world and Santa can't remember everything about everyone, can he? That'd be impossible. That's why he has his list of all the names, right? So he can remember?"

"I guess so," Aisling said.

"That means if he doesn't have the list then he's not going to remember who's been good and who's been bad. And if he doesn't know who's been good or bad, he'll just give presents to everyone cos he's a kind old guy."

"Oh no," Aisling said.

"Oh no, what?" Joe asked.

"You didn't," Aisling said.

"Didn't what?" Joe said. "Someone tell me what's happening."

"I think Victor's saying that when he

disappeared in Hanrahan's he snuck into Santa's grotto and . . ."

Victor reached inside his coat pocket and took out a piece of rolled-up paper tied up with a glittering red ribbon. It shimmered like starshine.

". . . he took Santa's List."

Chapter Thirteen

J oe's mouth dropped open. He couldn't believe it, but there it was right in front of him. Victor had done it, he'd actually done it.

"That's crazy! We'll go to jail for this."

"What are you talking about? Why would we go to jail?" Victor asked.

"You stole Santa's List!"

"I didn't steal it. I borrowed it and I'm going to give it back on the day after Christmas."

"I don't believe it. We stole from Santa Claus. We're actually the worst children ever,"

Joe said, flapping his arms in panic. "And I don't mean in a good way."

"Would you stop talking about stealing. We didn't steal. We borrowed," Victor said, his face turning a bright beetroot colour. "Can't you tell the difference?"

"Shhhh," Aisling said.

"Would you stop shush—"

But then they all heard it. The sound of Mrs Grough stirring upstairs. And everyone immediately shut up. For a minute they remained still like statues; the only sign they were alive was their icy breath in the cold night air.

When all was quiet again and they were certain Mrs Grough had fallen back asleep, they continued to talk in furious whispers.

"I thought you'd be happy," Victor said. "If he doesn't have the list, then he's not going to know the names of the kids that shouldn't be getting their presents. That means you'll actually have the Christmas you wanted."

"I think it's a good idea," Aisling said.

Victor beamed.

"No, it's a terrible idea. The worst idea I've ever heard. Possibly the worst idea that ever existed. We have to give it back. We have to give it back right now," Joe said.

"Maybe we should have a look at it first and then we can decide," Aisling said.

There was a gleam of mischief in her eye that Joe had seen before. It was this particular gleam that often led to trouble in the house and it was the last thing he needed right now.

"What? No way."

"This is Santa's List. His actual list. Don't you want to see if our names are on it? Aren't you even a teeny bit curious?"

"Curious? Don't you know what curiosity did to the rat?"

123

"No, what?"

"I don't know, but it must have been something really bad or they wouldn't have a saying about it. Do y—" Joe couldn't believe what Victor was doing. "He's opening it. He's actually opening the list."

Victor, with a surprisingly light touch, pulled on one end of the ribbon. The knot slipped away with a whisper and as he placed the ribbon on the table the list began to sparkle and swirl and unroll by itself. When it had been tied up with a neat bow it looked as if it must have been a short list, two or three page lengths' worth at most, but now they saw it went on and on and on. One ever-growing stretch of paper that was elegantly weaving its way around the kitchen.

Victor held one end of the list between his thumb and forefingers – the paper was rich and so very soft to the touch – as the rest of it kept unfurling, and then, as if by even stronger magic, it was across the kitchen table, under and over the chairs, almost but never quite touching any surface. A list that had looked like it could only hold fifty names now appeared to have hundreds and thousands, maybe even millions.

The writing was golden and the penmanship beautiful to behold, but they couldn't read any of the names. It was as if it was written in a language they didn't understand. And seeing Santa's List didn't panic them; it had the opposite effect – they felt calm and relaxed and peaceful.

"It's beautiful," Aisling said.

Joe and Victor were unable to speak, but they had smiles on their faces. This was like nothing they'd ever seen before.

Just when they thought it might keep on going for ever, the list stopped unfurling. It began to

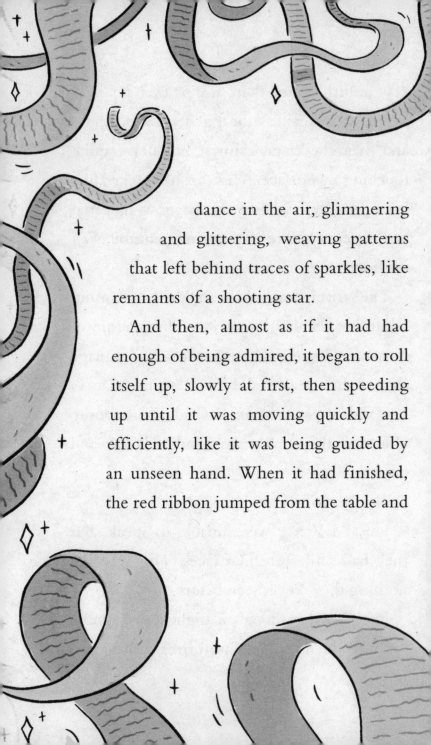

dance in the air, glimmering and glittering, weaving patterns that left behind traces of sparkles, like remnants of a shooting star.

And then, almost as if it had had enough of being admired, it began to roll itself up, slowly at first, then speeding up until it was moving quickly and efficiently, like it was being guided by an unseen hand. When it had finished, the red ribbon jumped from the table and

wrapped itself around the paper in a perfect bow before the list dropped itself back into Victor's coat pocket.

"Yeah, you know what, maybe you're right, we shouldn't hang on to this. I think the best thing to do is to give it back," Victor said.

Before anyone had the chance to reply, he took off again through the open back door, racing down the garden and leaping over the fence into Mr Quigley's yard.

"Why is he running—"

"What are you two doing in the kitchen after lights out?" Mrs Grough thundered.

She was standing in the kitchen doorway in her floor-length tartan dressing gown, slippers and hairnet.

How did she get down the stairs so quietly? Joe wondered. Even Hudson hadn't heard her. She's like a ninja ghost, he thought.

Mrs Grough bustled across the kitchen and shut the back door.

"And letting all the heat out too. Well, explain yourselves."

"We, ah, well, you know, we thought Hudson might be lonely so we came down to tell him a . . . bedtime story."

"Tell a dog a story? Utter nonsense. Back to bed now – it's the middle of the night."

"Middle of the night? It's quarter past nine,"

Joe grumbled as they headed back upstairs.

Aisling didn't sleep well that night. She had too much on her mind. Seeing the list had changed something in her. Before, she'd been worried about not getting presents, now it was different. The last thing she wanted to do was upset Santa. Victor had meant well, but he shouldn't have taken the list, Joe was right about that (there was a first time for everything). Of course, he wouldn't have taken the list at all if she hadn't asked for his help, so she was responsible really, wasn't she?

Still, none of this would have happened if Mrs Grough hadn't written to Santa in the first place, so if it was anyone's fault, it was hers. But thinking about Mrs Grough only led to her thinking about the damaged suitcase. That was Mrs Grough's fault too though, wasn't it? If she'd allowed Hudson to stay indoors then Aisling wouldn't have snuck him into the house and her beloved suitcase would be perfectly fine now. Yes, that was it, it was all Mrs Grough's fault.

So why did Aisling feel so guilty about it then?

She had to stop thinking about Mrs Grough; the list was more important. After all, she wasn't even sure Victor had taken the right list. There had been far too many names on it. Surely there weren't that many people in the world writing to Santa Claus to get children put on the bad list.

And then it struck her. What if it was a list of everyone who was going to be receiving presents? What if the list had all their names and addresses and what presents they were supposed to get? What if by taking the list they'd accidentally stopped all the other children in the world from getting their presents? What if Santa Claus didn't know where to go and what to give because of what they'd done?

Oh no, Aisling thought, this is a disaster. They'd end up ruining Christmas for everyone. They had to find a way to get the list back to Santa tomorrow. They just had to, then everything would go back to normal and all the children around the world would get their presents. All the children, except her, and maybe Joe.

No, she didn't sleep well at all.

Joe, on the other hand, slept like a log.

Chapter Fourteen

The following morning was Christmas Eve. Aisling, barely able to keep her eyes open from lack of sleep, ate her watery porridge, then asked Mrs Grough for permission to take Hudson for a walk.

"Another walk? You'll walk the hind legs off that dog," she said. "You can take him when you've done your chores. They should only take about three hours, four if you go too slowly."

She noticed the upset look on Joe's and Aisling's faces.

"Why are you two looking so miserable? It's only a bit of hard work. And your parents will be home later tonight. You should be happy. Or are you sad because you're going to miss me when I've gone?"

Then she added:

"That was a joke, by the way. I do have a sense of humour, you know."

"Good one, Mrs G . . . I mean, Mrs Grough," Joe said. "I'm laughing on the inside."

After their chores had been finished it was time for lunch, and it was well past one o'clock before they left the house. They were moving so quickly that Hudson could barely keep up with them.

"Do you think Victor's kept the list safe?" Aisling asked.

"Who knows what he's done. He could have eaten it, made the world's biggest paper plane out of it, he could have done anything. Don't forget about all the crazy stuff he's done at school."

"Yes, but we only heard about most of it. Maybe the stories weren't all true. Everyone says he's terrible, but he's nice enough at times. And Hudson really likes him. Name one crazy thing Victor's done since we met him."

"Apart from going to Santa's grotto and stealing a list that no child in the history of the world has ever stolen before?"

"Apart from that, yes," Aisling said. "OK, maybe you've got a point. Let's run faster."

They arrived at Victor's house in double-quick time and knocked loudly on the door.

It was flung open by a huge man wearing a ripped T-shirt and tracksuit bottoms. Joe wondered how he'd managed to open the door because he had a huge burger in one hand and he was picking his nose with the other.

"Whaddyawant?" he grunted.

"Is V-V-Victor here?" Joe stammered.

135

"Whowantstoknow?"

Joe hadn't a clue what the man had said. The words had just gushed out of him all at once, like it was one big long word rather than four words smashed together.

"We're his friends. From school," Aisling said.

The man was so confused his speech slowed down.

"Friends? Victor hasn't got any friends," he

said before shrugging and shouting so loudly that Hudson jumped about thirty centimetres into the air.

"VICTOR," he roared as bits of the burger flew from his mouth. "Somekidsheretoseeya."

He didn't invite them in, so they stood on the doorstep in the cold until Victor arrived. They knew immediately that there was something up. His eyes were red-rimmed and watery and for once Joe didn't feel in the least bit threatened by him.

"I thought you'd never get here," Victor said. "The worst thing ever has happened. I lost it. I lost Santa's List."

Chapter Fifteen

"OK, no need to panic. I'm calm," Aisling said. "It's not that big a deal. We've just lost the list. No reason to panic. It's a long list, so it's probably got the names and addresses of all the children in the world, so nobody's going to get any presents tomorrow morning and it'll be all our fault, but no need to panic. I'm totally calm."

"You've mentioned panic an awful lot for someone who's totally calm," Joe said, but even he knew how big a deal this was. What if they'd messed up Christmas for everyone?

It didn't bear thinking about.

"When you say you lost the list, are you joking?" Aisling asked.

"No. I wish I was, but I'm not," Victor said.

"Do you mean you lost it and you were really worried, but then you found it again, cos that'd be really great if you did, you know, that'd be brilliant."

"No, I lost it and I looked for it and I couldn't find it and now it's still lost."

He looked like he wanted to say he was sorry, but he couldn't. Victor would rather eat a gigantic bowl of pink slime than apologize.

"OK, there's no need for us to freak out. Let's just think about this logically, one step at a time, then we'll come up with a plan on what to do next," Joe said. "First question: where did you lose it?"

"If I knew that, I'd have found it, wouldn't I?"

"Good point, good point. Well, that's me

done. I'm out of ideas," Joe said, a little more chirpily than the situation deserved. He took a handful of sweets from his pocket. "Anyone want a jelly? Might help us think."

They all took one.

"Where did you get these? I thought Mrs Grough cleared all the sweets from the house?" Aisling asked, chewing a purple jelly.

"Yeah, I found these in my pocket. They must have been there for months, but they tasted all right when I scraped the hairy stuff off them."

"You scraped hairy stuff off them?"

"I was hardly going to eat them with it still on. I'm not a disgusting human being, Ash."

The others spat out their jellies.

"What a waste," Joe muttered.

"OK, when you left our house, you had the list. Did you go straight home?" Aisling asked.

Victor thought about it. He shut his eyes as

if he was going over every step of the route in his mind.

"Yes," he said finally. "I went straight from your house to my house and I only made one stop."

"So you didn't go straight home. If you stopped somewhere then—"

"Oh yeah, I never thought of it like that," Victor said.

"You had one of the most important things in the world in your pocket and you didn't go straight home and lock it away in a safe or a filing cabinet. Makes perfect sense to me. Where did you go?"

"I went to ... I ... look, tell anyone and I'll ..." he began, as if he was about to threaten them, but then he seemed to think better of it. "I'll show you, but keep it to yourself."

He led them around the back of the houses, to where the little piece of woodland lay.

Aisling and Joe recognized it as the spot they'd hoped to make a landing on the day they'd been carried in the air with Hudson. It looks a lot different from the ground than it does when you're on an out-of-control kite-parachute, Joe thought.

They spotted a sage-green wooden bird table fixed to an ash tree. It was clearly home-made. It was clunky and chunky and slightly misaligned; the paint was too thick in some places, too thin in others, but it had a certain charm to it.

"I built that," Victor said. "I feed the birds."

He almost sounded ashamed when he said it.

Joe didn't understand why Victor wanted his bird-feeding to be kept a secret, but Aisling did.

If people knew the toughest kid in school was kind to little birds then maybe they wouldn't think he was that tough after all.

There were thin broken branches piled on the ground in a fifteen-centimetre-high circle around the tree trunk.

"Why are there all those branches around the tree?" Joe asked.

"It's a warning system. Mr Grindle's cats are always trying to get at the birds and I thought if I put the branches there the cats would make a noise when they tried to sneak up and it would warn the little birds and give them a chance to escape. I came here last night cos I put the bird feed out so they'll have it in the morning. They get up a bit earlier than I do."

"Does anyone else come here?"

"No, only the cats."

"Wait," Joe said. "What if you dropped the list when you were here last night and

Mr Pringles—"

"Mr Grindle."

"Yeah, him, what if he came looking for his cats and he found the list and brought it back to his house and—"

Victor and Aisling were running towards Mr Grindle's house before Joe had even got halfway through his sentence.

"Well, that's great," Joe said, scoffing another formerly hairy jelly. "Looks like it's just you and me, Hudson."

But now Hudson had taken off too, skittering over the ice-topped snow.

"I wish everyone would stop running off while I'm talking," Joe called out. "It's very rude."

Chapter Sixteen

Victor banged on Mr Grindle's door with his fist, then used the metal door knocker while Aisling pressed the doorbell repeatedly.

Bang. Clank. Ding-dong. Thump. Clank. Ding-Dong.

"Mr Grindle!"

They made such a racket that some of the other kids in the neighbourhood ventured out of their houses to have a look at what was going on. They gathered around in twos and threes, some eating buttery toast from a two o'clock breakfast, others scoffing a cheeky Chomp or Freddo they'd snuck from a selection box when their parents weren't looking.

The letter box flicked open.

"Stop banging on my door or I'll call the gardaí," Mr Grindle said. All that was visible of him were his eyes, made larger by the thick milk-bottle lenses of the glasses he wore.

"We know you have it," Victor said.

"Have what? Charm and devastating good looks?"

"The list, Santa's List," Aisling whispered, not wanting the watching audience to hear. "Give it back and we won't make a fuss."

The letter box snapped shut as Joe caught up with them, more than a little out of breath. He waved a cheery hello to Willow, a girl from his class who lived in the yellow house across the street.

Mr Grindle was now peering out from

behind his net curtains. They could see at least seven cats perched near him. He squeaked the window open a scooch, just enough for his nose to poke out.

"List? What list? I don't know what you're talking about. Please leave my property at once, you trespassing, good-for-nothing . . ."

"Idiots?" Joe said.

"Yes, idiots," Mr Grindle concluded.

"Don't help him, Joe," Aisling said.

The window slammed shut, but just as soon as it did it was open again.

"Of course, it is a remarkably interesting list," Mr Grindle said. "And it appears to me that if a certain Mr S Claus doesn't have it in his possession by tonight, then there will be a lot of miserable children around the world tomorrow morning. Millions and millions of upset children. I can't think of a nicer Christmas present. It makes me so, so happy."

"Why would people being upset make you happy?" Aisling said. "That's just weird."

"Weird? Weird? How dare you! Why shouldn't it make me happy? Nobody ever gives me presents. Nobody visits me. If I'm miserable, then everyone else in the world should be miserable too," Mr Grindle said, adding an unnecessary cackle for good measure. He nodded at the children gathering on the streets. "Look at those poor innocent fools, delighted with themselves because it's Christmas Eve and they think Santa's calling tonight. Greedily waiting for all the presents their little hearts desire. They don't even realize how upset they're going to be tomorrow when they wake up to absolutely nothing. You know what, I think this is the best day of my life and it's going to get even better. Those young saps are going to help me keep the list out of your clutches."

"Yeah, really? Why would they do that?" Victor said.

"Just watch."

Mr Grindle opened the window a little wider and shouted out to the fifteen or twenty children watching on.

"Hello, neighbours. As you know, I can't stand any of you. Just seeing your stupid faces makes my stomach curdle, but seeing as it's Christmas, let's do something Christmassy. The first ones to hit my young friends here with ten snowballs shall win the princely sum of fifty euros. You heard me – fifty euros! What are you waiting for? Attack!"

And then he shut the window again, chuckling to himself.

"Don't worry," Victor said. "I know all these people. They're my neighbours too. They're not going to attack us with snowballs. They know how tough I am so they wouldn't dare."

The first snowball whizzed by his head moments later, missing him by centimetres.

"What the—? Oh no, you didn't, Hawk Willis!"

The second snowball splattered on Mr Grindle's window sending the cats watching from inside the house hissing and yowling and leaping around.

The third one hit Joe right plum on the nose. He fell to the ground a little too dramatically.

"Get up, you twerp, and start making snowballs," Aisling said.

She'd already made two.

"Oh, all right," Joe said, jumping to his feet.

A perfectly round snowball smacked Victor right in the face. He swept the crushed snow from his cheeks. "You're going to pay for that, Mumbles Doherty."

But before he could take action it was raining snowballs. They arced through the air like a volley of arrows, showering them from all sides. Hudson decided the best thing to do was to stay out of it until it was over. He snuck behind Mr Grindle's bins.

"We're outnumbered. What do we do?" Joe shouted as he took one to the shoulder, then the leg.

The snowballs thudded into the walls,

splashed on the ground and exploded against the bins (much to Hudson's displeasure).

"Attack," Aisling yelled. She grabbed an armful of the snowballs she'd made and ran out the front gate towards her new enemies, roaring like a warrior with nothing to lose.

"Yaaaaaaaarggghhhhh!"

The neighbours were taken aback by her ferocity and paused for a moment, unsure of what to do. They'd expected an attack from Victor, not this small girl. Aisling slung a snowball and it hit Mumbles on the side of the head.

"My ear, my beautiful ear," he cried.

Thud! Another one splatted into a girl twice Aisling's size.

"I knew there was something I liked about your sister," Victor grinned, before tearing after her, flinging snowballs left and right. He had a powerful throw and the snowballs stung when they connected, which caused some of those gathered to scatter in fear. The spirits of those who remained fell when they saw their neighbour with the terrifying reputation racing towards them.

"Retreat, retreat," they called out. "Loozer's on the rampage."

"The closer he gets the bigger he looks," said a boy who seemed astonished by the notion.

"Well, I'm not going to be the odd one out," Joe said, running after them, even though he'd only managed to make two snowballs in the time the others had made ten.

He yelled too, in a way he hoped was loud and terrifying but was closer to the sound of a mouse breaking wind. Then, as he tried to leap in what he considered a heroic manner, he tripped over the garden wall and landed flat on his face, leaving the imprint of his features in the snow. He got up quickly, carrying on as if nothing had happened, when he realized nobody had seen him fall.

Hudson barked his encouragement but remained exactly where he was.

"No fifty-euro note is worth this," cried Hawk Willis before he sprinted off into the distance, showing an impressive turn of pace.

The snowball fight was now three against five and as they continued flinging snowballs at each other, some landing, some missing wildly, a strange thing occurred. They forgot their cares and worries and Mrs Grough and their parents and the list. Instead they were simply happy. Their fingers were icy cold and there was snow on their faces and up their sleeves and melting ice down the backs of their shirts.

All at once Aisling burst out laughing. Great, joyful peals of laughter. Victor looked at her and laughed too.

And then the snowball fight was over. They'd won.

Chapter Seventeen

Hudson emerged from his hiding place, not even slightly ashamed of his earlier cowardly behaviour. There was no time for the children to celebrate. They had to get the list back from Mr Grindle. They banged on his front door again, but there was no reply. Then, for the second time in the last hour, Joe had a good idea.

"What if he's using the snowball fight as a distraction and is escaping out the back of his house?" he said.

That was exactly what Mr Grindle had

been doing. He'd left via the back door at the beginning of the snowball fight, hoping to slink away and disappear before the annoying children figured out what had happened. Unfortunately for him, a combination of his old age and the slippery conditions meant he'd only made it as far as the postbox located exactly thirty-seven metres from his house.

"They'll never catch me," he said, chuckling to himself.

"We already have, Mr Grindle. We're right behind you," Victor said.

Mr Grindle turned and saw it was true. They were only a couple of metres away. He wasn't going to give up without a fight, though.

"Officer," he cried, waving at the postbox. "These young hooligans have attacked me. Arrest them."

"That's not a garda," Joe said.

"It's not?" Mr Grindle said, squinting. "Well, then, whoever you are, fetch me an officer of the law."

"It's a postbox, Mr Grindle."

"What? Where are my glasses?"

"They're in the pocket of your dressing gown."

"Why are you being so helpful, Joe?" Aisling asked.

"I like him."

"You like Mr Grindle? Nobody likes Mr Grindle," Victor said.

"Yes, I have done my absolute best to be unlikeable," the old man said.

"You're not boring. Most grown-ups are polite and say things like 'look how much you've grown' and 'how was school today?' You don't, you just say all the mad things that come into your head. I like that."

"Enough talking. All we want is for you to

give us our list back," Aisling said.

Mr Grindle stroked his chin, as if he were deep in thought. "See, that's the thing. It's not your list, is it? It belongs to Mr Claus, so Cornelius Grindle has just as much right to have it in his possession as you do."

"We're not keeping it. We're going to give it back to Santa," Aisling said. "Give us the list. Please."

"Please, eh?" Mr Grindle said. "You'll have to be more polite than that."

"Pretty please?" Joe said.

"Why not try *Pretty please with sugar on top, and a nice iced biscuit with a red gumdrop*," Mr Grindle said.

The three children stared at him.

"Do you want the list or not?"

They all said the rhyme at the same time, Joe enthusiastically, the other two a lot more quietly: *Pretty please with sugar on top, and a nice iced biscuit with a red gumdrop.*

"Now, can we have the list back?" Aisling said.

"No," Mr Grindle said. "I just wanted to see if you were stupid enough to do what I asked."

"If you weren't so old, I'd punch you on the nose," Victor said, then turned to Joe. "You're not supposed to punch old people."

"You're not actually supposed to punch *anyone*," Joe said.

"This isn't the time for jokes," Victor said.

"I wasn't joki—"

"You're the meanest person I ever met," Aisling said.

"The meanest and the cleverest," Mr Grindle said. "So clever, I no longer have the list. I secured it in a locker at a secret location and I attached the key of that locker to the collar of my smartest cat – Mrs Pushkins von Whiskersons the Third. She's highly trained and obeys my every instruction. While you were engaging me in pointless chit-chat Mrs Pushkins was running away from here as fast as her feet would carry her."

"No," Aisling said.

"Oh yes," said Mr Grindle. "That cat is smarter than most humans and by now she is at least five miles away. The list is gone and Christmas has officially been ruined. You can search high and low, but you will never find her. Never in a million years."

A particularly fluffy, slightly overweight black-and-white cat emerged from the woods and trotted towards them, miaowing for attention. Around its neck was a collar and hanging on the collar was a key.

Chapter Eighteen

"It's Mrs Pushkins von Whiskersons the Third," Joe shouted excitedly.

"We know. We all see the key," Aisling said.

"Fly, my pretty, fly," Mr Grindle said, waving his spindly arms in the cat's general direction.

The cat, as cats often do when given instructions, completely ignored him.

"Well, Mr Grindle, it looks like you didn't win after all," Victor said. "We're going to get the list and we're going to give it back to Santa and Christmas won't be ruined." He turned to Aisling. "I only took it to help you. I don't want to wreck Christmas for everybody."

"Neither do I. I want everyone to enjoy it. Even if it means we have to pay the price," Aisling said.

"*Even if it means we have to pay the price*," Mr Grindle mimicked in a babyish voice. "You lot make me sick. What kind of lily-livered do-gooders are you? I've had a lot of bad Christmases and I *do* want everyone else to have a terrible time this year. I want everyone to be as miserable as I am. Miserable, cold and wretched. Now, come here, Mrs Pushkins."

He lurched forward to grab his cat.

But he was far too slow. Victor got there before him and was just about to pick up the cat when Hudson decided to help. The little dog raced forward barking and yelping, terrifying Mrs Pushkins, who leaped up before spinning in mid-air and then racing off down the road as fast as she could, her feet barely touching the ground, the key still dangling from her collar.

Hudson looked up at Joe, tail wagging, tongue lolling out, waiting for the praise and treat he was certain was going to come his way.

"Hudson, I love you, but sometimes I think you're the worst dog in the world," Aisling sighed as Mr Grindle whooped and celebrated.

"Yip," Hudson agreed.

"In your face," Mr Grindle said. "There'll be no Santa Claus visit this year and it's all your fault."

✦ Chapter ✦ Nineteen

"**I** think I saw which way that cat went. Follow me," Victor said.

"No, wait," Aisling said. "We need help."

She didn't want to ask an adult for assistance. She never had before. The only grown-ups she ever wanted help from were her parents and if they weren't around she always managed perfectly fine by herself. But this was different; this wasn't just about her.

"We can't waste time looking for the cat on foot. It could take for ever to find her. The list has to be back in Santa's hands tonight so we need someone who can help track her down quickly. Someone with skills. Someone who can drive."

"Do we know anyone like that?" Joe said.

"Do we . . . Mrs Grough!" Aisling cried.

"Oh yeah, she was in the army and she's trained for loads of things. I forgot that."

"Wait, you want to ask that scary woman for help? Wasn't she the one who wrote to Santa in the first place? The one who told him not to bring you anything for Christmas?" Victor said.

"Really? She sounds delightful," said Mr Grindle, who appeared to be happy enough to hang around and enjoy the children's misfortune.

"Why would she help you, Aisling?" Victor continued. "And if she wrote to Santa for letting a dog eat a mouldy old suitcase, what would she do if she found out that we might be ruining Christmas for every kid in the world?"

"She'd mangalize us," Joe said. "Wait, is mangalize a word? If it's not, it really should be. Anyway, she'd definitely do something we wouldn't like."

"That's a chance we have to take," Aisling said. "Even if it means trouble for us."

If Mrs Grough was surprised to find three red-faced, sweaty children and a yapping dog bursting into the kitchen all at once she didn't show it. And to the children's surprise, she didn't immediately start complaining about the noise or the fact that they hadn't immediately taken off their shoes. Instead, she lowered the heat on the bubbling pot of cabbage, took off her apron and sat down.

"Tell me what's going on," she said.

Aisling was the first to recover her breath.

"Promise you won't get mad," she said.

"I won't promise that."

"OK. But if you are mad and you want to punish us can you do it later, because if you punish us now it's bad news for everyone."

"And she means everyone," Victor said.

"Yeah, like the entire world," Joe said.

"You two boys should remain silent now. Aisling, go ahead," Mrs Grough said.

Aisling quickly told her the whole story. Mrs Grough pursed her lips early on and they remained pursed throughout.

"So you see, Mrs Grough," Aisling said when she'd finished the tale. "We have to find Mr Grindle's cat, get the key to the locker, then get the list and give it back to Santa. And we have to do it all before midnight."

Aisling thought she might have to do more to persuade her babysitter, but to her surprise she didn't.

"I'll help you," Mrs Grough said. "And since

time is a factor, I suggest we leave immediately. Your parents are due home in less than two hours."

"We're going to be the kids that saved Christmas," Joe shouted.

"If we fail we'll be known as the kids that ruined Christmas," Victor said.

"Oh yeah, that's not as good."

Due to Hudson's previous reaction to Mrs Pushkins von Whiskersons the Third, he wasn't allowed go with them. Instead, they left him in front of the stove with some leftover broiled chicken and his favourite chew toy.

"You can stay inside for now, but I'll be talking to you later," Mrs Grough said to Hudson, who wagged his tail in reply, either not understanding or not caring. She turned to the children. "I'll be talking to all of you later too."

Joe gulped. He didn't like the sound of that.

Mrs Grough ushered them outside while she packed supplies into a large green rucksack none of them had seen her use previously.

Before they left, her phone rang. It was an ancient mobile as large as a brick and unable to even connect to the internet. She pressed a giant green button.

"Hello? Oh yes, Mr Gilligan, good to hear from you. Yes, everyone's happy and healthy. We're just about to sit down in front of the fire and play a lovely game of Monopoly."

Joe turned to Aisling in surprise. Had Mrs Grough just lied to their dad?

"I'm terribly sorry to hear that, but these things happen," she said. "What's that? You'd like to speak to the children. Of course— Oh no, the phone's battery is dying and I can't see the charger anywhere."

Another lie! Who was this imposter who'd come in and replaced Mrs Grough?

She held the phone out in front of her. "Children, say a quick hello."

"Hello," Aisling, Joe and Victor shouted.

Mrs Grough gave Victor a disapproving look, then got back on her mobile. "Yes, that did sound like three children, rather than two. It must be due to a strange echo on the phone. Better go. Fly safely, bye, bye, bye."

She ended the call.

"Your parents' flight has been delayed. They won't be back until tomorrow morning," Mrs Grough said.

At any other time the news that their parents were staying away for another night would have upset them, but all Aisling and Joe could think of was that it gave them more time to find Santa.

It was dark now, but the town looked cheery with its twinkling Christmas lights and covering of snow. Since Mrs Grough didn't have a car of her own, she borrowed Aisling and Joe's mother's car. After a quick call to Victor's dad to let him know where he was – he hadn't even realized his son wasn't at home – they all squashed in.

"You have been behind the wheel of a car before, haven't you, Mrs Grough?" Joe asked. "I mean, you don't have one of your own, so—"

"I was one of the first female rally drivers in the country," Mrs Grough replied. "Now, buckle up, kids. I drive fast."

Chapter Twenty

The car shot off like a rocket and the children were slammed back into their seats by the huge G-force generated. Mrs Grough swerved the car down the road, forcing a man out jogging to leap into a nearby garden.

"First, we're going to find Mr Grindle," Mrs Grough said. "Until then, Aisling, eyes right. Joseph, eyes left. I'll watch the front, and Victor, you take the back. Any sign of a black-and-white cat, let me know. We're moving fast, so if you think you see something don't mumble, shout. Understood?"

There were a few half-hearted answers from the back of the car.

"I asked if I was understood."

"YES, MRS GROUGH," they all shouted in unison.

Within a couple of minutes, they'd reached Victor's estate. It was already dark and cold and there weren't many people on the streets. Most were locked away in their houses, eating sweets and mince pies by roaring fires, some playing board games, others exploring new worlds on their consoles or watching films from years gone by.

There was no answer at Mr Grindle's, so they swung around the road at the back of his house and spotted a hunched figure wandering about, dressed in warm winter clothing, including a scarf and a faded black overcoat.

"That's him," Aisling said.

Mrs Grough hit the brakes, then executed a handbrake turn, sending the car sliding sideways across the icy surface before it stopped right beside Mr Grindle. She pushed open the passenger door.

Mr Grindle's eyes were red and he looked as if he'd been crying.

"Oh, it's you," he said when he spotted the children. "Get lost."

"Hello, Mr Grindle. My name is Mrs Grough. I am a babysitter to two thirds of the children you see and temporary guardian of the third. Since you're wandering around here in the cold and dark, I presume you haven't found your cat, and since it's mainly an indoor cat you're worrying about it being outside at night."

"Just like Hudson," Aisling grumbled.

"You want to get your pet back, Mr Grindle, and we want the key on its collar, so we're going to work together."

"I'm not—" Mr Grindle began.

"I don't want to hear it. We don't have time to waste. Get in the car, Mr Grindle," Mrs Grough said. "Get in now."

To the children's surprise he obeyed immediately.

"Now, listen up, lady and gentlemen," Mrs Grough said. "Our cat has been on the run for forty-three minutes. Average cat's foot speed is 3.5 km an hour. That gives us a radius of 2.5 kilometres. We're going to conduct a search of every petrol station, garden, henhouse and doghouse in that area. The cat's name is Mrs Pushkins von Whiskersons the Third. Let's go get her."

As the car took off, Mr Grindle smiled, almost as if he were glad to be part of an adventure.

"I like the cut of your jib, young lady," he said.

Aisling and Joe exchanged glances. Young? Mrs Grough?

"Do be a dear and shut up, Mr Grindle."

"Yes, ma'am."

They drove around for the next three hours without having any luck. Mr Grindle had grumbled, the children's tummies had rumbled and Mrs Grough had to drink from her coffee flask to stay awake. She'd used all the tools in her arsenal. They'd searched everywhere. They'd knocked on doors, clambered over fences and been chased on three separate occasions by angry dogs.

They'd driven all around the town. They'd managed to locate four other missing cats and returned them to their owners, but they hadn't managed to find the cat they were looking for.

At one point they thought they had. Victor had spotted a black-and-white cat on the roof of the sports shop. It looked exactly like the missing cat and he cried out.

"That's not her," Mr Grindle snarled. "Mrs Pushkins' front left paw is two centimetres longer than her front right paw. That cat's paws are clearly of an even length, you idiot."

"You're a cantankerous old man, aren't you?" Mrs Grough said.

"Thank you."

"That wasn't supposed to be a compliment."

It was nine o'clock already; time was running out and spirits were low. Unless something changed they weren't going to succeed.

"We can't spend any more time driving around.

It'll soon be Christmas morning and it'll be too late to return the list to Santa. Let's just smash open the locker and grab it," Victor said. "It's not like stealing or anything; it is your locker."

"It is my locker, but I'm not telling you where it is," Mr Grindle said.

"Well, then I'll smash open every locker in town. It's a proper emergency so it's not really a crime or anything. I can do it, I'm super strong."

"Yeah, and he'll do it with his fists," Joe said. "They're called Deathkiller and The Punisher!"

Victor looked at him, wondering what Joe was talking about.

"Nobody's smashing anything. We are not interfering with other people's personal property. And that's the final word on the matter," Mrs Grough said. "We will find the cat and then Mr Grindle will give us Santa's List. He's going to do it because despite being exceptionally rude and mean, he has a caring side."

"No, I don't," Mr Grindle said sulkily.

"Really? How many cats do you have?"

"Twelve."

"You look after all of them, don't you? And here you are late on a cold Christmas Eve night looking for one of them. Why would you do that unless you cared about something other than yourself?"

"That's weird," Joe said. "Sorry for interrupting, but I just saw Jiggles the Elf."

"The grumpy elf from the shopping centre?" Aisling said. "It's not that weird. He's probably spending the night in Santa's grotto. Might be out for a walk to get some fresh air."

"No, the weird thing is that he was carrying an open tin of cat food."

Chapter Twenty-One

Mrs Grough reversed the car at speed, zigzagging along the snow-slushed street until they were right beside the elf. If he was surprised to see them, he didn't show it.

"Hello, Jiggles. Are you going to feed a cat?" Aisling asked.

"No, this is my supper. After a long boring day at work I like nothing better than slumping in front of the TV and eating a delicious tin of cat food. Now, please leave me alone, strange little child."

He began to walk away.

"Wait," Aisling said. "Does the cat you're feeding have a key hanging from its collar?"

Jiggles paused. His eyes narrowed. "Maybe it does and maybe it doesn't."

"And did anything strange happen at work yesterday?"

"Why are you asking so many questions?"

"Please, Mr Jiggles. This is important. Anything strange at work yesterday?"

"Yes, there was some sort of emergency. Everyone was running around in a panic, all stressed out. Nobody told me what it was about, of course. Jiggles never gets told anything."

Aisling smiled. "Jiggles, how would you like to be known as the elf that saved Christmas?"

"Wouldn't mind it, I suppose. Beats hanging around here. I'm not saying this town is boring, but . . . wait, no I am saying it's boring, so yeah,

sure, anything's better than this."

It wasn't the enthusiastic answer Aisling had been hoping for, but it would have to do.

"Is that really an elf?" Mr Grindle asked, his eyes wide with astonishment, as Jiggles climbed into the back of the car.

"No, I just dress like this because it's so fashionable," Jiggles said.

It was a tight squeeze in the back seat and the bobble of Jiggles's hat was practically stuck up Victor's nose. The car was soon filled with the pungent odour of cat food.

"Stop here," Jiggles said after they were driving for less than a couple of minutes.

They were beside a dark alley that ran alongside the red-bricked town hall. At the end of the alley was a padlocked iron gate that was almost two metres high.

"The cat's on the other side of that gate. She's hiding near some bins at the back. I heard her crying and mewling and I thought she might be hungry and that I could tempt her out with the food."

Mrs Grough parked the car and the six of them walked down the alleyway, guided by the light from Mrs Grough's flashlight. Victor carried her heavy rucksack to show everyone how strong he was.

"I don't think we should all climb the gate. It might spook the cat. Maybe just one person,"

Mrs Grough said.

"Me, of course," Mr Grindle said. "It's my cat."

"But I don't think you'll be able to climb—"

"I won't be able? What a stinking load of decaying rubbish. I'm only seventy-eight, you know." But when he tried it proved too much for him and he turned to Aisling. "Yes, that is a bit high. Can you go? I really want to see my cat."

Aisling didn't need to be asked twice. Without any help, she clambered over the gate and dropped down carefully on the other side. Jiggles passed her the cat food through the bars and Mr Grindle offered her his scarf.

"It has my scent on it. Mrs Pushkins will recognize it."

Aisling walked slowly towards the bins, then dropped down to her haunches and stretched out her arm, the palm of her hand directed towards the cat's hiding place.

"Here, Mrs Pushkins. Psh, wsh, wsh."

She heard a miaow, a plaintive little cry.

"Sing her a song. She likes songs, especially Abba," Mr Grindle said.

Aisling wasn't going to sing in front of everyone, not a chance. She moved forward and laid the open tin of cat food on the ground, then took a few steps back again. After a minute or two, Mrs Pushkins peeped her head out from behind the bins. Everyone held their breath.

"It's OK, my little friend. I'm not going to hurt you," Aisling said.

Mrs Pushkins hesitated, then took another couple of steps forward, passing the tin of food, until she was just in front of Aisling. She rubbed the side of her head against the leg of Aisling's jeans, then allowed her to gently stroke her head before Aisling picked her up. Mrs Pushkins began to purr and nuzzled into her neck.

Mr Grindle reached through the bars of the gate, desperate to be reunited with his cat.

"Don't give her to him," Joe shouted. "If Mr Grindle gets the cat back he won't tell us where the locker is and we'll never find the list in time."

Aisling looked at Mr Grindle. He was mean enough to take the cat and never tell them where the locker was. But she could see the joy in his eyes at the idea of being reunited with Mrs Pushkins. She couldn't hold her hostage. She was many things, but she wasn't a catnapper.

"You're probably right, Joe, but I can't do it. Here you go, Mr Grindle," she said, carefully passing the cat through the bars of the gate.

Mr Grindle gently tucked Mrs Pushkins under his arm. He didn't say *thank you* or *in your face, loser* or *ha, ha, Christmas is ruined*. Instead, he said something Aisling hadn't expected him to say.

"Santa's List is in locker number 227 at the railway station."

Victor raised his hand to high-five Mrs Grough but stopped when he saw the look of disapproval on her face.

"Not a high-five person, huh?" he said. He turned to Joe. "Your sister did it!"

"Did what?" Joe asked.

Chapter Twenty-Two

Mr Fleming, the stationmaster, had been enjoying a late light snooze when he was awoken by the sound of two adults, three children, one elf and a cat rattling around the otherwise empty railway station.

"Hey, what's going on over there?" he called out as they raced, walked and limped towards the locker area.

"We're trying to find a magical list and save Christmas for millions of children," Aisling shouted.

"Well, can you do it a bit more quietly.

I'm trying to get some sleep," he said before returning to his little office.

The lockers were arranged in neat rows, piled on top of each other, three high. Victor, Aisling and Joe immediately began looking for number 227. They didn't have to look for long. Locker 227 was the only one lit up from the inside with sprinkles of light dancing around its edges.

"I found it. It's in there," Joe said unnecessarily.

"Wow, great work, kid. You know, with brilliant investigative skills like that you really should set up your own detective agency," Jiggles said.

"Thank you?"

They waited impatiently for Mr Grindle to arrive and open the locker. He made a big production of it too, taking the key from Mrs Pushkins' collar with a great flourish, until Mrs Grough snapped at him.

"Oh, do get on with it, Mr Grindle," she said.

Aisling held her breath as the locker creaked open.

And there it was, hovering in mid-air in a golden haze of flickering magic: Santa's List.

Once again, the children felt a sense of calm and peace when they saw it, as if everything was all right in the world.

"Now, all we have to do is find Santa Claus, who could be absolutely anywhere on the planet on the busiest night of the year, give him the list of all the children who are getting presents, hope he's not too cross with us and then get back home before our parents find out what we've been up to," Joe said.

"You don't have to worry about the last part," Mrs Grough said. "I'll be telling your parents exactly what you've been up to tomorrow morning."

"Happy Christmas to you too, Mrs Grough," Joe said.

Once they'd climbed back into the car Mrs Grough drove with purpose, although nobody seemed to be sure where they were going or what they were going to do when they got there.

"What's happening?" Joe whispered.

"I don't have a clue, but I don't think she does either. The elf should know how to get in touch with Santa," Victor said. "Don't you know where his sleigh is?"

"As I might have mentioned before, I've never actually been on Santa's sleigh. Not even once. It's quite a sore point because, unlike some people I could mention, I'm not the sort of elf who wants to spend his time sitting on a shelf, so thanks a lot for bringing it up," Jiggles said.

"But don't you have some sort of magic way of talking to him or something?" Victor said.

"No, you're thinking of wizards. They're the ones with the magic. Hey, do you want me to get in touch with my friend Frank the Wizard? He might be able to help us," Jiggles said.

"You have a friend who's a wizard?" Victor asked, astonished.

"No, I don't. I was being sarcastic. Do you know why? Because there's no such thing as wizards!"

"Wizards? Told you those kids were idiots," Mr Grindle said. "Shhh, back to sleep, Mrs Pushkins. You've had such a long day, haven't you, my poor little thing."

Within moments, he was snoring himself.

They had left the town behind and were now driving along quiet country roads.

"I don't know where I'm going," Mrs Grough said. "I hoped that if I kept driving some kind of plan would pop into my head, but nothing has."

"I have an idea," Aisling said.

✴ Chapter ✴ Twenty-Three

"It might not work, but it's the best chance we have," Mrs Grough said, when Aisling explained what she had in mind.

They were driving down a country lane so narrow that the car was scraping the ditch on both sides of the road at the same time. In the absence of street lights they could see thousands of stars high in the pitch-black sky. The grass in the fields was hidden beneath a crisp layer of white. As they got further along the road, it grew steeper and steeper and the car began to slip and groan as it struggled up the hill. Mrs Grough stopped the car, consulted her map, then took out a compass to check she was going in the direction she wanted.

Finally, just as the car's engine was whining so much it sounded like it was about to fall apart, they reached the end of the road. They were at the very top of a hill that overlooked the town which lay far below, nestled cosily in a valley. Its twinkling lights made it seem warm and safe and Christmassy, but Aisling was too filled with anxiety to enjoy the sight.

"What are we doing all the way up here in the middle of nowhere?" Mr Grindle asked when he woke up.

"We're trying to attract Santa's attention and the higher up we are the better chance he has of seeing us when he passes in his sleigh," Aisling said.

"He's never going to spot us here. Believe me when I tell you this Christmas it won't be *ho, ho, ho*, it'll be *oh no, no, no*," Mr Grindle said.

"Don't be so negative," Mrs Grough said. "Don't listen to him, children."

They clambered out of the car and she gave each of them a flashlight, which they duct-taped to the roof, back and sides of the car so that every lens was pointing towards the sky. They switched on all the flashlights and the beams shone upwards like a signal to anyone flying overhead. Then Mrs Grough switched on the car's headlights.

"What now?" Joe asked.

"Now, we cross our fingers and wait," Mrs Grough said.

She opened her rucksack and produced a flask of piping-hot oxtail soup, several cups and some plain cheese sandwiches. Everyone was so hungry that the whole lot was demolished in five minutes.

After an hour and a half the chatter died down. It was approaching midnight.

"Is anyone cold? I've got some blankets," Mrs Grough said, reaching into her rucksack again.

"How much can fit in one rucksack? It must be magic," Joe said to Victor.

Mrs Grough handed out the tartan blankets and they wrapped themselves up in them until they were toasty and warm. Mr Grindle was lying on the back seat of the car,

Mrs Pushkins asleep on his chest, as the car gently shook to the sound of his snores. Jiggles sat on the bonnet, Santa's List gripped tightly in his little fist.

As they sat there, the minutes ticking by, hoping against hope that they would spot the great man and the reindeer in the night sky, Aisling had time to think. What if they failed? She'd be responsible for ruining everyone's Christmas. Every child in the world would hate her.

"You won't, you know," Mrs Grough said, taking a seat beside her.

"What?"

"You're worried about ruining Christmas, aren't you? Well, you won't."

"But if all the children don't get their presents . . ."

"They'll get over it. Oh, they'll cry and wail and stamp their feet and make a big fuss, but they'll get over it in the end. People are resilient. Presents are nice, but they're just the cherry on the top of the cake."

"Tell that to my brother. If he doesn't get his Soccer Blaster X, he'll go crazy."

Mrs Grough smiled. "When I was a child, I really, really wanted a Cindy doll for Christmas. It was extremely popular at the time. I didn't get it. And I cried for two days straight."

"And then you were OK?"

"No, I was bitter about it for months, years afterwards. It still hurts sometimes."

"That's not helpful," Aisling said, stifling a yawn.

"But the world didn't end because I didn't get it. And I went on and had lots of fun and a great life afterwards. I did things I'd never thought I could do and that meant more than any doll ever could . . ."

Aisling had fallen asleep, her head slumped against Mrs Grough's shoulder. When she looked around, Mrs Grough noticed that Victor and Joe had fallen asleep too even though they had both seemed wide awake only a couple of minutes earlier. That's odd, she thought, but then she heard the jingle of sleigh bells in the night sky.

✷ Chapter ✷ Twenty-Four

Aisling wondered if she was dreaming. She was exhausted, her eyes stuck together with sleep, but she could hear him. Santa Claus. Was he really here?

Then she heard Mrs Grough's voice. "Hello, Santa," she said.

"Hullo, Mrs Grough. It's been a long time since we last met," said Santa. "How kind of you to help return my list."

"You're welcome. I don't know how it happened. I must have picked it up absent-mindedly when I visited your grotto."

"Yes," Santa said with a twinkle in his eye. "That's what must have happened. You were probably at the grotto hoping to retrieve the letter you wrote when you were angry."

"I regretted writing that letter as soon as I popped it in the postbox."

Aisling couldn't believe her ears. Mrs Grough was pretending that she was responsible for taking the list and she was even admitting she was sorry for writing the letter. She was trying to keep them out of trouble!

"You've made mistakes, the children have made mistakes, but then everyone makes mistakes, don't they? We're only human and it's impossible to get everything right," Santa Claus said.

"I'm here too, Santa," Jiggles said.

"Hullo, Jiggles, my friend. How good to see you again. I've heard wonderful things about you."

"You have?"

208

"Oh yes. I know how busy you've been and how hard you've worked. Thank you."

"You're welcome, Santa. Happy to do it," Jiggles said. And he meant it too.

"I'm afraid though, Jiggles, that I have a small favour to ask. I hate to burden you on Christmas Eve, but due to our … delays, shall we say … I need a helping hand tonight. Would you mind?"

"You mean … you mean … go on the sleigh with you?"

"That is exactly what I mean."

"I'd love it. I'd love it. I'd love it," Jiggles said, leaping off the car bonnet and clicking his heels in delight.

Aisling dared to open one eye, just a little. She saw Santa reach out, take Jiggles by the hand and lift him gently into the sleigh that was hovering two metres above the ground. There was a golden bag filled with presents

behind him and out in front were the reindeers. There was Rudolph with his red nose. Was that Dasher and Prancer and . . .

Santa turned towards her. Aisling shut her eyes again. She knew that she wasn't supposed to see him now, not when he was delivering presents. She tried to go back to sleep, but there was something gnawing away at her, an uncomfortable feeling in the pit of her stomach. She may not have liked Mrs Grough very much, but it wasn't fair to let Santa think that everything was her fault, was it?

She heard the car door open, followed by footsteps crunching on the snowy hilltop. She peeked once more. It was Mr Grindle.

"S-S-S-Santa?" Mr Grindle said. Seventy of his seventy-eight years seemed to fall away and for a moment the joy on his face made him look like a young boy again.

"Hullo, Cornelius," Santa said. "It's been a long time since we've seen each other."

And then Mr Grindle, feeling lighter and happier than he'd felt in years, said something he'd never said to anyone before.

"I-I-I'm lonely . . ."

"I know, Cornelius, I know. Everything will be all right, but you must ask for help when you need it. Most people are nice. They want to help others. Promise me you'll ask."

"I promise, Santa."

"And that you'll be nice in return," Santa said.

"Well, I can't promise that, but I will try," Cornelius Grindle said.

"That's a start," Santa chuckled. "Now, time is against me and we must be off. Are you ready to go, Jiggles?"

"I've never been more ready for anything in my entire life," Jiggles squealed.

"Goodbye, Cornelius; goodbye, Mrs Grough," Santa said.

This was it. Aisling knew she was going to get away with it. Mrs Grough had taken the blame and Aisling was going to get her presents. That was a good thing. But then why did she feel rotten about it? If Joe was awake he'd have gone crazy over what she was about to do. She could hear his voice in her head, telling her to just continue pretending to be asleep and everything would work out fine.

"Santa, wait," she said.

She opened her eyes, fully this time, and

stood up.

"About your list. It wasn't Mrs Grough's fault. It was mine. I'm the one responsible for taking it. Nobody else," she said.

"Nobody else?" Santa said.

"Well, let's just say none of it would have happened if it wasn't for me."

"Let's just say that then," Santa smiled.

Aisling walked over to his sleigh. "Can I ask you something?"

Santa leaned down and she whispered into his ear. He smiled again, happy with what she'd said. He sat upright and waved to Mr Grindle, Mrs Grough, the two sleeping boys and Mrs Pushkins, who was peeping out from the car.

"This time I really must go. Merry Christmas, everyone," Santa Claus said.

And with that the reindeers galloped across the sky, smoothly pulling the sleigh and showering sprinkles of stardust behind them.

✦ Chapter ✦ Twenty-Five

"You should have woken me up," Joe complained. "I can't believe I didn't get to meet Santa Claus. What did he look like?"

"You met him two weeks ago. He looks exactly the same," Aisling said.

"I knew it."

"I wish I'd seen him. I could have said sorry for borrowing the list," Victor said.

"You mean you could have said sorry for stealing the list," Joe said.

"I BORROWED IT!"

"There was no need. Santa hardly mentioned it."

Mrs Grough looked into the rear-view mirror, caught Aisling's eye and winked. It was like they had their own little secret now.

They dropped off Mr Grindle, Mrs Pushkins and Victor at the door of their houses.

"I hope you won't get into any trouble for being so late, Victor," Mrs Grough said.

"Nah, they'll hardly have even noticed that I was gone," he replied, getting out of the car. He looked a little downbeat now that their adventure was over. "Guess I'll see you two when we're back at school."

"Unless . . ." Aisling began.

When she saw Victor's face light up with hope, she knew she had to say it.

"If you like, you can call around to our house tomorrow."

"Maybe I will if I've got nothing better to do," Victor said, trying to play it cool, although Aisling knew by the way he said it that he'd definitely be there.

"And maybe I'll ask for that favour you owe me too, Joe," Victor said.

"That's it. I'm going to die tomorrow," Joe muttered to himself.

"Can I come to your house too?" Mr Grindle said. He didn't look Aisling in the eye. His head was down, as if he was embarrassed for even asking. "I know I don't really care for any of you, but I don't want to be on my own on Christmas Day."

"Of course, Mr Grindle, you can come with Victor. He knows where we live," Aisling said.

Mr Grindle was so pleased he almost smiled. With that, they said their goodbyes and Mrs Grough drove in the direction of home.

"You do realize that you just invited the meanest man we've ever met and the toughest kid in school to our house on Christmas Day," Joe said.

"And you did so without asking your parents' permission," Mrs Grough added.

Aisling didn't reply. She just stared out of the window at the falling snow.

Chapter Twenty-Six

"Well," said Mam as the car pulled up on the driveway on Christmas afternoon. "That was the worst business trip I've ever been on. A complete and utter disaster. Once we've seen Aisling and Joe, all I want is to have a nice hot bath followed by some peace and quiet."

"Yes," Dad agreed. "I'd like a roaring fire, a belly full of chocolate and some games with the kids. That would be heaven. I know we probably went a bit over the top hiring a super-strict warrior babysitter, but it's worth it just to get home to a clean, peaceful house."

They opened the front door to be greeted by their worst nightmare. Their entire home was in chaos. Hudson was fighting with a little white deer ornament on the Christmas tree and managed to bring the entire tree crashing down after a tug of war. The crash frightened Mr Grindle's cats and eleven of them raced across the hall floor and up the stairs at top speed.

"It's that dog of yours again. He's a menace," they heard Mr Grindle shout.

Cornelius Grindle appeared in the hallway, his chin smeared with gravy and some bread stuffing peeping out of the pocket of his best blazer.

"Thieves. Burglars. Trespassers!" he shouted.

"We're not thieves. This is our home," Dad said.

"Well, learn how to control your dog then," he said, hobbling up the stairs after the cats,

who from the ripping sounds above sounded like they were in the middle of shredding some bedroom curtains.

"Who was that?" Mam asked.

"I have absolutely no idea."

They heard music blaring from the kitchen and opened the door at the most unfortunate moment. Mrs Grough was dancing by herself.

"You were right, Mr Grindle. I quite like this Abba group. Are they new?" she roared.

Seeing Mrs Grough dancing wasn't the unfortunate part.

"Food fight," Victor yelled, flinging some soggy mashed potato across the kitchen. Aisling and Joe ducked, but their parents weren't as quick and the mash was a direct hit. As the buttery potato slid down their faces and on to their clothes, Mrs Grough spotted them.

"Oh, hello there. Did you have a nice trip?"

*

Aisling and Joe had patiently waited until their parents arrived for present time, but it took a while longer before their mam and dad had calmed down enough to be in the humour for opening Christmas gifts. Coming home to chaos meant they were certain their children had broken another babysitter, but when they realized that Mrs Grough was quite happy to babysit again, their mood improved. Joe's mood disimproved when he opened his presents to find out he didn't get what he wanted. Not even close. He sulked for almost an hour. Aisling didn't get what she wanted either, but for once she smiled and made the best of it.

When Mr Grindle and Victor had left with their bellies full and the cats trailing behind them, Mrs Grough announced she was leaving too.

"But it's Christmas night. You can't go back to an empty house on Christmas night. You have to stay here with us," Mam said.

"I'm perfectly happy spending some time by myself," Mrs Grough said with a smile. "There's a big difference between being alone and being lonely."

She packed her belongings into the green rucksack and some black bin bags.

"Where's your family heirloom suitcase?" Dad asked.

Aisling and Joe looked at each other. Despite what she'd said the night before, Mrs Grough hadn't actually reprimanded them at all. In fact, she'd been nice. Joe didn't understand it, but Aisling thought it might have had something to do with her owning up to being responsible for the list fiasco. Still, that was last night, this was today. Here comes trouble, Aisling thought.

"Oh, the case finally fell apart after all these years, so I put it in the bin. I'll have to get a new one once the shops open after Christmas."

She hadn't said anything about the trouble they'd caused or the adventures they'd been wrapped up in. Aisling couldn't believe it. First, she hadn't blabbed to Santa, now this. Did Mrs Grough like them? And, more worryingly, was she starting to like Mrs Grough?

"Hudson!" Dad shouted in despair.

The little dog had brought the Christmas tree crashing down once again.

"I think you're right, Mrs Grough. Dogs should be kept outside," Dad said.

As Dad fixed the tree, he noticed a large rectangular present right in the corner. It hadn't been opened yet. Somehow, they'd missed it earlier. He read the name tag.

"It's . . . it's for you, Mrs Grough."

He didn't remember buying the woman a present and from the look on his wife's face she hadn't bought it either. He knew Aisling and Joe hadn't a penny between them and even if they had, they weren't going to spend it on their babysitter.

Mrs Grough unwrapped it carefully, as if it was the most precious thing in the world. It was a suitcase, but it wasn't brand new. It was almost exactly the same as the one Hudson had half eaten.

"How is that even possible," Joe gasped.

It's magic, Aisling thought.

Hudson greedily eyed up Mrs Grough's present.

"Don't even think about it," Aisling said to the little dog, who seemed slightly miffed at his fun being spoiled.

There were tears in Mrs Grough's eyes. "It's the most beautiful thing I've ever seen," she said.

"But isn't that the same suitcase she had the day she arrived?" Dad whispered.

Mam nodded. "It looks exactly the same to

me," she whispered in reply.

"I thought she said it was broken. That's what she said only five minutes ago, right? And why would someone wrap up a suitcase she already owns? There's something very strange going on here," Dad said.

"Dancing, cats, strangers in our house, Aisling being pleasant. It's all very weird," Mam replied.

As Mrs Grough lifted the suitcase up for closer inspection, she noticed it rattled. "There's something else in there."

She unsnapped the latches and lifted the lid. Joe gasped. And for once Aisling didn't complain about him being dramatic. She gasped too.

Inside the suitcase were the two presents they'd wanted most: an Electric Robot Dancer and Soccer Blaster X.

Joe grabbed his present and, overcome

with joy, began to sprint around the house.
Aisling wasn't as excitable. She was happy to
get the present, but for some reason it wasn't
as important as it had been three days ago. She
noticed a note inside. She opened it up and
read it.

Santa said the only present the annoying girl asked for was this suitcase, that she didn't want anything for herself. How very noble of you, Aisling (and yes, i am being sarcastic). But if you three children hadn't been so foolish, i'd never have got to ride in Santa's sleigh so the two presents inside the suitcase are from me to say thanks for being such bubbleheads. i've left another present under the tree of the angry boy. He'll get it when he goes home. Oh, and Santa says hi. —Jiggles the Elf.

"Yeeeeeeeeeeessssss," Joe shouted. "Best Christmas ever."

Acknowledgments

I am extremely grateful to the following people for their help with *The Santa List*.

To Yasmin Morrissey, my editor, for all her enthusiasm, support and hard work. To Ruth Bennett, who expertly guided the book through its later stages. Thanks to James Lancett for his fantastic illustrations which really brought the characters to life. To Aimee Stewart for her amazing book design. To Jessica White for copyediting and to Susila Baybars for proofreading. Thanks to both of you for catching all my mistakes. And thanks, as always, to my brilliant agent, Marianne Gunn O'Connor.

Finally, a big hello from Kieran & Deirdre to our good friends Lera and Lida.

Dear Mr Santa Claus

My name is Joe. You probly know that already. I've been good all year. Well, most of the year anyway. Well, some of the year. I've been good for at least a month. I know some people say I have not been good at all but you shud ignoor them. Beeng good is not easy when your a kid but I've really really tryed. I really have.

This is what I'd like for Christmas:
1) Soccer Blaster X (coz it's brilliant).
2) One big surprise or lots and lots of small surprises.

If you can't think of any surprises then you could leave some money like 2000 euros or something and I could buy presents myself. I know your busy so that mite make it easier for you.

Have a great Christmas, Santa. I hope you get to relax and put your feet up in the fire.

From your friend
Joe

Dear Santa

I hope you're happy. I would like an Electric Robot Dancer for Christmas this year. I know it's a lot to ask, so I don't want any other presents. I would like it if you could make it so that my parents didn't have to work so hard, though. I know that's not really a present so maybe you can't do anything about it, but they're always tired and we don't really get to do any fun family stuff any more. Instead, we get all these babysitters who are OK I suppose, but it's not much fun having strangers in your house all the time.

If I could have one last wish (I've asked for three now and I know you're not a genie) then it would be to make my brother Joe less annoying. It's not his fault that he's a giant pain I suppose, it's just the way he is. But even if you made him 300 per cent less annoying, he'd still be 1000 times more annoying than most people. If you spent time with him then you'd know exactly what I mean. Anyway, see if you can do anything to help. Thanks.

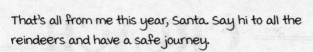

That's all from me this year, Santa. Say hi to all the reindeers and have a safe journey.

Lots of love
Aisling x

THE CARRAIG CRUACH GAZETTE

A local paper for local people

Each week we interview a member of the community for our feature *My Favourite Things*. This week it's the turn of Mrs Grough, a former army sergeant and current babysitter.

Hello, Mrs Grough. It seems very formal to call you Mrs Grough. Can I ask you what your first name is? You can ask, but you won't get an answer. Please address me as Mrs Grough, young man.

Oh, OK. Do you have any favourite sayings? Yes. If you're not the early bird, then you're the worm. **I'm not sure that makes sense and...** It makes perfect sense. It means get up early in the morning and don't lie in bed until 7.30 a.m. like all the lazy people. And talking of lazy, stop slouching in your chair like that and sit up straight.

Sorry. What's your favourite way to spend a Sunday?
Up at dawn, a quick six-mile run, some porridge for
breakfast, then tidy the house from top to bottom, power-
wash the driveway, clean all the windows, polish three
pairs of shoes, read a book, do some press-ups. A relaxing
Sunday like that is my idea of heaven.

Favourite place for a holiday? I wouldn't waste my
money on a holiday. What's wrong with staying at home?

Favourite book? *The Giant Book of Exceptionally Tough
Army Exercises.*

Favourite possession? A watch. Timekeeping is the most
important thing in the world. I can't abide lateness.

Favourite TV programme? I don't own a television
or a computer.

Favourite song? Have you heard of the pop group
Abba? Their music is very catchy.

Favourite colour? What a ridiculous question.
Nobody over the age of two should have a favourite
colour. Utter nonsense.

THE ICE SCOOP

Photo by James Lancett

Each week we hear what it's really like behind the scenes in the lead-up to Christmas in our feature:

A Life in the Day

Jiggles the Elf was born and raised in the North Pole. He began his career looking after reindeer before joining Santa's Workshop where he worked in the board games section for many years. He was promoted to Assistant Toymaker (Fourth Class) under the leadership of the legendary Twinkles McSparkle, who annoyed Jiggles on an hourly basis due to her relentlessly cheery nature and ability to turn every negative into a positive. For the last five years Jiggles has divided his time between the North Pole and various department stores around the world, where he works as an assistant in Santa's Grotto.

I wake up early as elves don't need much sleep. I have a light, healthy breakfast of berries, yoghurt and seven mince pies. Some elves exercise in the morning, which is a perfectly fine thing to do if you've got straw for brains. The younger ones look ridiculous as they wear leggings and headbands and fancy trainers when they go for a run. What's wrong with good old-fashioned pointy-toed shoes?

If I'm in the North Pole I might go and have a chat with the reindeer. Rudolph's the superstar, yet he's got far too big for his boots if you ask me. Dasher's the funny one – he's hilarious – but if you want all the gossip then you've got to talk to Blitzen. The reindeer always tease me because I'm one of the few elves who hasn't accompanied Santa on his sleigh on Christmas Eve, but that's fine. I'm a good sport about it and it's not something I'd ever mention. I don't like to complain!

My afternoons at the grotto are a lot different from my days in the North Pole. That's when you get to meet the children. Santa and Mrs Claus love children. 'They're our greatest treasure,' Mrs Claus says. I agree with that, especially if the word treasure means annoying, spoilt, pukey, ignorant, rude, little pipsqueaks. When we close the grotto for the night I tidy up and prepare for the next day, then I wash my uniform (thanks for throwing candyfloss and slushees at me, you lovely treasures). Mrs Claus gives me lots and fruit and vegetables for dinner, so I say thanks very much before sneaking off for a pizza. I love pizza. After dinner, I put my feet up and read a good book. When I go to bed, I'm so tired that I fall asleep as soon as my head hits the pillow.

About the Author

Kieran Crowley is a children's writer from Cork in Ireland. He has written a number of books including *The Mighty Dynamo* and *The Misfits Club*. He decided to write a story set around the visit of Santa Claus as when he was growing up Christmas Eve was his favourite day of the year (his birthday and FA Cup final day were his second and third favourites).

About the Illustrator

James Lancett is a London based illustrator, director and yellow sock lover! As a child growing up in Cardiff he was obsessed with cartoons, video games and all things fantasy. He moved to London to study BA Illustration and Animation at Kingston University. This degree opened the door to a job he had dreamt of ever since he was a kid and he now works as an illustrator and animation director.